TROUBLE IN JULY

OTHER BOOKS BY ERSKINE CALDWELL

God's Little Acre
Tobacco Road
Kneel to the Rising Sun
We Are the Living
Journeyman
American Earth
Southways

WITH MARGARET BOURKE-WHITE

You Have Seen Their Faces
North of the Danube

ERSKINE CALDWELL

TROUBLE
IN JULY

DUELL, SLOAN & PEARCE
NEW YORK

PRINTED IN THE UNITED STATES OF AMERICA
BY QUINN & BODEN COMPANY, INC., RAHWAY, N. J.

For Janet, Dee, and Pix

TROUBLE IN JULY

CHAPTER I

SHERIFF JEFF MC CURTAIN was sound asleep in bed with his wife on the top floor of the jailhouse in Andrewjones, the county seat, when the noise of somebody pounding on the door woke him up. He was a heavy sleeper, and only an unusually loud noise, or a shaking by his wife, ever made him wake up before daylight in the morning.

He and his wife lived in four comfortable rooms on the second story in the front section of the red-brick jailhouse. The rooms directly underneath on the first floor were offices, and behind them was a long barn-like room filled with ceiling-high prisoners' cages. There was a heavy iron-grid door, and also a thick steel fire-door, between the two parts of the building. The law required the sheriff of the county to maintain his permanent residence in the jailhouse, because there he would be in a better position to guard the prisoners.

Sheriff Jeff McCurtain did not mind living there,

3

because it was rent-free and the rooms were airy in summer and warm in winter. His wife, Corra, though, was a little ashamed of having to live under the same roof with prisoners. Every time she spoke about it, Sheriff Jeff told her that the people on the inside were no different than those on the outside, except that they had been caught. The prisoners in the jailhouse were generally a handful of Negroes who had been caught passing counterfeit dimes and quarters, a few who had shot up a Saturday night church social or fish-fry merely for the fun of it, and every now and then two or three bail-jumpers of both races.

The pounding on the bedroom door stopped for a while, and Sheriff Jeff lay awake listening to hear if whoever it was had gone away. It angered him to be roused up like that out of a sound sleep in the middle of the night. He had gone to a lot of trouble to select reliable deputies who could take care of anything that came up during his sleeping hours. Besides, there was only one prisoner in the jailhouse. He was a Geechee Negro named Sam Brinson, who was being held, as usual, for having sold a mortgaged secondhand automobile. The old car was not worth more than eight or ten dollars, at the most, and Sheriff Jeff was getting ready to turn Sam loose in a few days, anyway.

4

Corra turned over and began shaking him.

"Jeff, there's something the matter," she said, getting up on her knees and working over him as she would over a washboard. Corra was a little woman, weighing less than a hundred pounds. She was a match for him when she could use her tongue, but she knew it was useless and a waste of breath to try to talk to him when he was asleep. Sheriff Jeff was a large man. He was tall and bulky and heavy. He weighed in the neighborhood of three hundred pounds, although in winter he ate more and added fifteen or twenty pounds of seasonal weight. Corra got a good grip on his neck and shoulder and went at him as if he were a pair of mud-stained overalls. "Wake up, Jeff! Wake up this very instant! Something's wrong, Jeff!"

"What's wrong?" he asked sleepily. "What time is it in the night?"

"Never mind the time. Wake up like I tell you."

"A man's got a right to his sleep no matter what office he holds."

She shook him a little longer for good measure.

"Wake up, Jeff," she said. "Wake up and stir yourself."

He reached out and turned on the light. He could see his watch on the table under the lamp without having to raise his head. It was a quarter past twelve.

"If that Sam Brinson has broken jail, and one of those deputies came up here and woke me up at this time of night to tell me about it, I'm going to—"

"Shut up, Jeff, and stop that fussing," Corra said, releasing her grip on his flesh and sitting back on her heels. "This ain't no time to be quarreling with the deputies or anybody else. Something may be wrong somewhere. Almost anything is liable to happen at this time of night."

There was another outburst of noise at the door, louder than before. This time it sounded as if somebody had started kicking the door with his foot. Some of the houseflies on the ceiling woke up and came down to the bed.

"Is that you, Bert?" Corra asked in her high-pitched voice. She got up erectly on her knees, clutching the pink silk nightgown over her thin chest. "What's the matter, Bert?"

"Yes'm," Bert said. "I hated to wake up Sheriff Jeff, but I thought I'd better."

Sheriff Jeff slapped at a ticklish housefly that was crawling across his forehead. The exertion made him wider awake. He turned over and sat up on the side of the bed. He moved slowly, his heavy weight making the springs and wooden bedstead creak as if they were going to give way under the strain.

"What's got into you at this time of night, Bert?" he shouted, fully awake at last. "What's the sense of making so much noise in the middle of the night like this? Don't you know I need my sleep? How can I wake up fresh in the morning if my night's rest is all broken up?" He slapped savagely at another fly. "What's the matter?"

Corra got up and ran across the room with her little short strides. She took her yellow-flowered wrapper from the hook behind the door and slipped it on.

"What do you want with Mr. McCurtain, Bert?" she said, coming back to the bed, drawing the wrapper tightly around her, and sitting down.

"Tell him I think he'd better get dressed and come downstairs right away, Mrs. McCurtain," he said uneasily. "It's important."

"That's the trouble with political life," Sheriff Jeff said, mumbling to himself. "Everything's important till you look it straight in the face. Once you look at it, it's pretty apt to turn out to be something that could have waited."

"Stop your grumbling, Jeff," Corra said, digging her elbow into his side. "Bert says it's important."

7

"Them smart-aleck deputies, Bert and Jim both, think it's something important every time a nigger's caught robbing a hen-roost."

"You get up and get dressed," Corra said, jumping to her feet and standing before him with a cross look on her face. "Do you hear me, Jeff?"

He looked up at his wife and slapped at one of the flies tickling the back of his neck.

"Bert!" he shouted. "Why didn't you wait till daylight? If you've got a new prisoner down there, lock him up and I'll attend to him the first thing in the morning after I've had a chance to eat my breakfast."

He waited for Bert to say something. There was silence outside the door.

"And if one of you smart-alecks has gone and picked up a nigger gal bitch laying-out in an alley, and come and woke me up like this to tell me about it, I'm here to tell you I'm going to do something far-fetched. I want them nigger gals left alone, anyway. There's been too much fooling around with them back there in the cage-room all this summer. I'll fire both of you deputies quicker than a dog can yelp if you don't stop it. If you can't stick to white gals, you've got to go somewhere else to do your laying-out with the nigger ones. Tell Jim Couch I said—"

"Jefferson!" Corra said sharply, her voice jabbing him like a pin-prick.

"Well, hot blast it, I want it stopped!" he said roughly.

"It's nothing like that at all this time, Sheriff Jeff," Bert said quickly. "You'd better come down right away."

"Did Sam Brinson break jail after all I've done for him?"

"No, sir. The Brinson nigger is still in No. 3. He's sound asleep back there."

Corra came and sat down on the bed beside him, drawing the yellow-flowered wrapper tightly around her body as though she would allow nothing of hers to touch him. She did not speak right away, but Sheriff Jeff knew by the way in which she looked at him that he was going to have to listen to a lot of talk from her before he left the room. He dropped his head in his hands and waited for it to begin. He could hear Bert going down the stairs.

"Jeff, you haven't had anything to do with those colored girls yourself, have you?" she finally asked, her voice rising and falling with inflections of tenderness and concern. "I'd die of humiliation, Jeff. I just couldn't stand it. I don't know what I'd do."

9

When she paused, he shook his head slowly from side to side. From the corners of his eyes he was able to glance at his watch on the table. He had listened to her on the subject so many times in the past that he knew just how long it would take her to say what she had on her mind. He dropped his head wearily back into the confines of his hands and closed his eyes peacefully. It was a relief to his mind to be able to close his eyes at a time like that and think of things far away.

"There was a colored girl locked up from last Saturday night until Monday morning, Jeff. Did you go down to the cage-room while she was there?"

He shook his head.

Corra had started in again when Bert suddenly knocked on the door again.

"Sheriff Jeff, you better come quick!"

"What's happened, Bert?" Corra asked, jumping up.

"It's some kind of trouble over near Flowery Branch. A nigger over there got into trouble and a crowd of white men has gone out to look for him. It looks pretty bad, Mrs. McCurtain. Don't you think Sheriff Jeff ought to get up and come down to see about it?"

Sheriff Jeff groaned miserably. It meant that he

would have to get up and dress himself and go fishing. He knew no man alive hated fishing as much as he did.

"Did you hear what Bert said, Jeff?" his wife cried, running to him and shaking him as hard as she could. "Did you hear that?"

He groaned from the depths of his body.

"I've grown old long before my time," he said sadly. "Holding political office is what has caused it. I'm nothing but a frazzle-assed old man now."

He got up, straining his legs while the weight of his body was becoming balanced, and reached for his clothes. He hated the sight of a fish; he never ate fish; and he would walk several blocks out of his way to escape the smell of one. But going fishing was the only means he had of escaping from a controversial matter. He had had to go away on fishing trips so many times during the eleven years he had been sheriff of Julie County that he knew more about worm- and fly-fishing than any man in that part of the world. He had had to force himself to catch fish in every known manner. He had snared them with a wire-loop; he had seined them; he had shot them with a rifle; and, when he had been unable to catch them any other way, he had dynamited them.

"Jeff," Corra said, "the best place in the world for

you at a time like this is down on Lord's Creek, fishing."

He turned on her, his lips spluttering.

"Hot blast it!" he shouted. "Why do you have to say 'fish' to me at a time like this when you know how much I hate it!"

"Now, Jeff," she said placidly. "Just try to control yourself a little."

"Are you coming, Sheriff Jeff?" Bert inquired meekly from the hall. "That nigger they're looking for is liable to get caught almost anytime now."

"Go on down to the office and wait for me, Bert," he said weakly. "I'll be down toreckly to see what I can do."

He got his feet through his pants legs.

"Now, mark my words, Jefferson McCurtain," Corra began. "If there ever was a time for you to go fishing, this—"

"Hot blast it till God-come-Wednesday!" he shouted, tugging at his pantstops and pulling the waistband over his belly. "Can't you see the fix I'm in! For eleven years I've worked myself frazzle-assed trying to keep from getting mixed up in political disputes just so I can keep this office. And now all you can do at a time like this is to fuss at me. You know this trouble is liable to split the next election wide open. Why do you have to torment me when I'm trying my best to figure what to do?"

"I'm only telling you for your own good, Jeff," she said tenderly, ignoring his anger.

He tried to hurry, but his movements were hampered by the necessity of keeping the weight of his body in balance. When it came to his shoes, Corra had to get down and guide his feet into them and then tie the laces.

"Mrs. McCurtain—" Bert said outside the door.

"He's getting dressed now, Bert. Go downstairs to the office and wait."

Jeff turned around several times, looking for his hat. Corra got it and put it on his head.

"I'll bet a pretty that all this hot-blasted trouble started about pure nothing," he said, gazing at his wife. "When the dust settles, it won't amount to a hill of beans. That's why I hate to waste my time waiting till God-come-Wednesday for things to straighten out."

"You let the people argue all that out among themselves," Corra told him. She raised her finger in front of her nose and began shaking it at him. "But I'm standing here telling you in plain words that if you

13

don't stay away from that end of the county, and go fishing somewhere for the next three or four days, you're going to regret it as long as you live on the topside of this earth, Jeff McCurtain. Now, you hurry on off to Lord's Creek like I told you."

He gazed longingly at the soft bed and at the hollow his weight had made. The springs and mattress sagged invitingly. When he tried to turn away from the sight of it, he found that his body had become more unwieldy than ever.

"I wish you had to go just once and sit all day long poking a stick into a creekful of slimy fish," he said. "The mosquitoes will eat big pieces out of me, and what's left of me will itch for the next two weeks with chigger bites."

"As sure as you are living, Jefferson McCurtain," Corra said warningly, wagging her head, "you'll lose the election this fall if you go one step nearer Flowery Branch than you are now. You managed to get reelected last time only because Judge Ben Allen was able to pull strings at the very last minute. If you get into a mix-up like a lynching or something, neither Judge Ben Allen or nobody else in Julie County will be able to get their hands on enough wires or ropes

14

to keep you in office. People are as shifty as the south wind in November when it comes to voting."

He put his watch into his pocket with his wife's warning ringing in his ears. Without waiting any longer, he moved heavily across the room towards the door. His large body made everything within sight look small and insignificant in comparison. The floor squeaked painfully under his weight.

When Corra saw him moving slowly across the room, she could not keep from feeling sorry for him. If she could get her hands on the person responsible for all the trouble, she would make whoever it was sorry he was ever born.

She ran to him when he put his hand on the knob of the door.

"Be sure and get that bottle of mosquito oil in the drawer of your desk downstairs," she urged, patting his arm. "It's the bottle you had with you the last time down at the creek. Be sure and rub it all over your face and neck, Jeff. The mosquitoes on Lord's Creek are worse this year than they have ever been. And take care of yourself properly, Jeff."

She squeezed his arm affectionately.

He left the room without looking back again. On the way downstairs he wished to himself that people who had it in them to do it would go ahead and do their lynching and tell him about it after it was all over. There was scarcely any political risk in coming along after the lynching had taken place and saying the law had to be enforced and upheld, because by that time, ninety-nine times out of a hundred, there was not a man to be found who would come forward and identify a member of a mob. But there was a handful of men and women in the county who always made it a point to remind him every time a lynching had been threatened during his eleven years in office that it was his sworn duty to protect the life of a suspect until he could be taken to trial before a court. The last time a Negro was lynched in Julie County, about six years before, he went fishing as soon as word reached him that a crowd of white men was looking for the Negro, and he had stayed down on Lord's Creek for five days. When he got back, the Negro was dead, and the whole thing had blown over and quieted down. But some of the people had accused him ever since of neglect of duty. It was those men and women who could cause a lot of trouble for him if another lynching took place in the county. It might even cost him his job this time.

"Bert!" he called, easing his weight down the stairs

first on one foot and then on the other one. "Do you hear, Bert!"

Bert came running from the office and stood at the bottom of the stairway.

"It looks bad, Sheriff Jeff," Bert said, following him through the hall and into the office.

"What does?" he asked, standing in the middle of the room and blinking his eyes sleepily in the bright light. "What looks bad?"

"That trouble out at Flowery Branch."

"What's the trouble about?"

"I haven't been able to find out much yet. I've been trying to ring up Jim Couch to see what he knows, but Jim's wife said he left home an hour ago and hasn't come back yet."

"I'm going to do something far-fetched to you and Jim Couch both, if all this turns out to be nothing but pure hullabaloo."

"They say a nigger boy named Sonny Clark raped a white girl out there about sundown last night."

The sheriff did not say anything for a while. He moved over the floor to his desk, picked up some papers and threw them down again.

"What's the white girl's name?" he asked without looking at Bert.

17

"Katy Barlow."

He sat down heavily in his chair at the desk. It was an especially large chair with arm rests made wide enough apart for the width of his body. He leaned back cautiously.

"Some of those folks up there in those sand hills beyond Flowery Branch raise girls that never have drawn the color line," he said. "It's not an easy thing to say about brother whites, but it has always looked to me like them folks up there never was particular enough about the color line. However, a nigger man ought to be more watchful, even if it is one of those white girls up there in the sand hills. If the niggers would—"

"That Barlow family lives up there," Bert said.

"But that ain't one of Shep Barlow's womenfolks, is it?"

"She's his daughter."

The sheriff's jaw fell ajar. He stared at Bert, shaking his head unbelievingly. Some of the papers slipped off the desk and fluttered to the floor.

"Man alive! Shep's daughter?"

Bert nodded.

"That's bad," he said after a while. "That's really bad. Shep Barlow ain't nobody you can fool with.

About nine years ago he killed a nigger for just accidentally breaking a hoe-handle. And only a few years before that he killed another one for a little thing a lot less. I've forgotten what it was now. Shep Barlow ain't one to stand for something like that, especially if it's his daughter that's been raped."

"That's what I've been trying to tell you ever since I called you the first time, Sheriff Jeff. I tried to tell you it was important. Jim Couch said—"

"But you didn't tell me it was anything to do with Shep Barlow," he said, pushing himself to his feet. "That makes all the difference in the world. There's going to be a mess of trouble as sure as the sun's going to rise tomorrow morning. There's bound to be trouble now."

He began filling his leather pouch with smoking tobacco from the glass jar on the desk. His hands were shaking so badly he spilled more tobacco on the desk than he managed to get into the pouch. When he had finished, he swept the spilled tobacco to the floor with a single motion of his hand.

"Maybe when Jim Couch phones in—" Bert began.

"Maybe, nothing!" he said, his voice shaken. "There ain't no maybe about it. Get me my fishing pole out of the closet. I'm going off fishing for a few days. While I'm gone, you and Jim look after things the best you can. But don't do nothing without proper orders from me. No matter who says what, you deputies ain't got the right to so much as turn over a stick unless I give the word."

"Yes, sir, Sheriff Jeff," Bert said.

Jeff pulled out three or four desk drawers, feeling inside of them for the bottle of mosquito oil. He found it and held it up between his eyes and the light globe. It was all of half full of yellowish fluid. He tamped the stopper tightly and dropped the bottle into his pocket.

"You can let Sam Brinson, the colored man, out in a few days, but tell him I said if he mortgages any old car again and then turns around and sells it over his head, I'm going straight to the courthouse and get a writ of estoppel drawn against him that'll tie him hand and foot. And I don't want to find that cage-room back there full of nigger wenches, either, when I come back. The last time I went off for a few days, I came back here and found a nigger gal in almost every cage in the whole jailhouse. You tell Jim Couch I said you and him has got to do your wenching someplace else after this. I ain't going to stand having this jail turned into a whorehouse every time I turn my back. If it happens again, I'm going to do something far-fetched to you boys."

"Yes, sir," Bert said.

CHAPTER II

WHILE Bert was looking in the closet for the fishing pole, Jeff McCurtain walked out on the front porch and looked up at the starry night. He felt lonesome the minute he left Bert and heard the screen door slam behind him. He knew he was going to spend four or five of the lonesomest days of his life down on Lord's Creek. He wished he could take Corra with him to keep him company, but he knew she would never consent to any such proposal.

He walked down the steps and looked up at the bedroom windows on the second story. The light was still burning, and he could see Corra's shadow moving around the room. He knew she was waiting up to make sure he left for the creek.

Just as he was turning to look at the stars once more, an automobile roared through the middle of town, coming down the main street at a fast rate of speed. At the corner a block away, the car slowed down suddenly with an ear-splitting shrieking of tires on the pavement. A moment later the headlights from the car turned the night in front of the jailhouse brighter than day. The automobile jerked to a stop, bouncing from end to end. Before Jeff could get out of sight, somebody jumped out and ran towards him.

"Sheriff Jeff!"

"Is that you, Jim?"

"I'm glad you're up and dressed, Sheriff Jeff."

"What's the matter?"

Jim Couch, the elder of the two deputies on the staff, ran up the walk. He was out of breath. He stood looking up at Jeff, panting for wind.

"I just came from Flowery Branch," he managed to say, his voice raucous with excitement. He stopped and breathed deeply several times before he could say anything more. "I thought maybe you hadn't heard about the trouble." He took a deep breath and cleared his throat. "I didn't want to stay out there and get mixed up in the trouble until I was certain what you're going to do about it, Sheriff Jeff."

Jeff looked down at Jim calmly and serenely.

"Me?" he said quietly. "I'm going fishing, son."

They walked up the brick path to the porch and opened the screen door. The phone in the office suddenly began to ring with a shrill, unpleasant clamor. Jeff went into the hall and stood in the office door. Bert had already picked up the phone.

"Is this Sheriff McCurtain's office?" a husky voice boomed.

"Yes," Bert said, his eyes turning slowly in his head until he was looking Jeff straight in the face. "Deputy Bert Stovall speaking."

"What kind of a sheriff's office are you folks running anyhow?" the voice demanded.

"What do you mean?" Bert asked, wondering who it was.

"You'd better get McCurtain up out of bed and tell him to get busy and catch a nigger named Sonny Clark, or I'll come to Andrewjones and jerk McCurtain out of bed myself. I want Sonny Clark caught and locked up for safekeeping. Do you hear me?"

"Who's talking?" Bert asked excitedly. "Who are you? What's your name?"

"This is Bob Watson at Flowery Branch. Sonny Clark has been accused of raping a white girl, the daughter of one of the tenants on my place. Sonny is one of my field hands. I don't want no trouble out here. If Sonny Clark gets lynched, there won't be a nigger left on my plantation by sundown tomorrow

24

night. Or if some of them don't run off, they'll be too scared to get out in the fields and work. My whole crop will be ruined. Don't forget this is laying-by time. I won't even be able to hire outside help if a nigger gets lynched out here. You tell McCurtain I said for him to get up out of bed and come out here and catch Sonny and take him to Andrewjones, or somewhere, and lock him up good and tight for safekeeping till this trouble blows over. I voted for McCurtain the last time he ran for re-election, and my wife votes the same ticket I vote. But he'll never get another vote in this part of Julie County if he don't come out here and do something right away before it's too late. He was elected and draws a bigger salary than he's worth to do just what I'm telling you now. You tell McCurtain I said he's already done enough fishing to last him a lifetime, and if he goes again now, it'll be just once too many. Good-by!"

Bert set the phone down carefully, fearful that it would burst into another clamor of ringing before he could get away from it. Crossing the room, he repeated to Jeff practically every word Bob Watson had said. Jeff listened with his mind in a ruffle, leaning his weight against the doorframe.

Nobody said anything for several minutes after

25

Bert had finished. Jim Couch stood behind Jeff in the hall, waiting impatiently for the sheriff to act.

Jeff moved his bulky body across the room and sat down heavily in the big arm-chair behind the desk. Jim followed him into the room.

"Jim," he said slowly, looking up at the deputy under drooping eyelids, "Jim, it's things like this that has whipped me frazzle-assed for eleven long years."

Both Jim and Bert nodded sympathetically. They realized he was at that moment in the tightest corner of his entire political career. On one hand there was a crowd of Julie County citizens, all registered and qualified voters, who would do their best to throw him out of office if he attempted to interfere with their lynching of Sonny Clark. On the other hand there was a small group of influential men and women, one of them being Bob Watson, who would do anything within their power to ruin him politically if he did not show some evidence of trying to stop the lynching.

"If it had happened anywhere else in the country," Jeff said wearily, "it wouldn't amount to so much. I can't figure out why that blame nigger had to be one of Bob Watson's hands. It's a pure shame."

Bob Watson was the largest landowner in Julie

County. He owned nearly half of all the farming land in the county, and almost all the timber land. He farmed about fifteen hundred acres of cotton with field-hands. Another fifteen hundred acres were let out to renters, sharecroppers, and tenants.

Corra came downstairs and stood in the doorway. She knew at once by the look on her husband's face that something unexpected had turned up to discourage him.

Bert went to the door and told her in whispers what had been said over the phone.

"I'm licked, Corra," Jeff said, looking at her helplessly.

"Nonsense," Corra said. "Bob Watson is nothing but bluff and bluster. You know better than to pay any attention to what he says. Haul yourself up out of that chair and get on down to Lord's Creek like I told you almost an hour ago. Get up from there and stir yourself, Jeff."

Jim Couch went out to the porch to wait. Bert stood ready to help Jeff get started.

"Maybe you're right, Corra," he said, taking heart. "It's sitting around here letting these things get me into a stew that does the damage. Bert, where's that fishing pole of mine? Get me what I need. I ain't got no more time to waste."

He got up and walked heavily towards the door. His wife followed him, patting his arm, until he reached the front porch. Throwing himself forward, he crossed the porch, went down the steps, and hurried towards his car standing in the street. At the sidewalk he turned around for a last look at Corra, but she had gone out of sight.

Jim had followed him down the brick path to the car.

"Since you're figuring on being gone four or five days," Jim began hesitantly, "I thought I ought to remind you about Mrs. Narcissa Calhoun, Sheriff Jeff."

"What about her?"

"Maybe you've forgotten about her. It's that petition she been getting up for the past two or three months. This is going to be a bad time, nigger-trouble coming right on top of that."

Jeff's shoulders sagged.

"That's right," he said, his gaze falling to the ground. "I'd clean forgot."

The light in the bedroom went out. Corra had gone back to bed, thinking he had left for Lord's Creek.

He looked up at the darkened windows for a while, trying to think.

"If she gets a majority of the voters to sign that petition, that might settle the election right there and then," Jim suggested.

Jeff nodded, his gaze still fastened upon the ground.

Mrs. Narcissa Calhoun was a grass widow about forty-eight years old who made a living selling Bibles and religious tracts. She had kept after Jeff to buy one of her books during all the past spring and summer, and he finally bought a tract with the hope that she would leave him alone after that. He had not seen her again until one morning three weeks before when she walked into his office carrying a big bundle of papers. That was when he found out that she was canvassing the county for signatures to a petition, the object of which was to send all the Negroes to Africa. She had written a letter to Senator Ashley Dukes and told him that the Negroes were buying Black Jesus Bibles from a mail-order house in Chicago, and that he would be as shocked and scandalized as she was to see pictures of Christ looking like a Negro. She told him something ought to be done right away to stop the circulation of Black Jesus Bibles in the nation. Senator Ashley Dukes wrote back and asked her what she proposed to do about it. Narcissa told him she wanted to get up a petition with millions and millions of names on it asking the President to send all the Negroes back to Africa where they came from. Senator Ashley Dukes wrote to her again and told her if she persuaded everybody in Georgia of voting age to sign the petition, he would act accordingly. That was the point when Narcissa started out to get everybody, white and twenty-one, to sign it. Jeff had told her the first thing that because he was in politics he could not sign his name to it. She kept after him so persistently that finally he promised to sign the petition if she got everybody else in the county to sign it first.

"That petition changes the complexion of everything," Jeff said, thinking hard.

"What are you going to do, Sheriff Jeff?" Jim asked.

"Sometimes I wish I was just a frazzle-assed beggar with nothing in the world to worry about except a bite to eat now and then," Jeff said dejectedly. "Being sheriff ain't what it's talked up to be, Jim. My soul is worried limp from one day's end to the next. I can't even remember when I've had a minute's pure peace. There's always something coming along to torment a man in politics. You no sooner get through one election than you have to turn right straight around and start worrying about the outcome of the next one. Voters are a queer lot of people. I've seen out-at-the-front candidates wind up at the tail-end for a little thing like not wearing a pair of galluses. Now, ain't that pure discouraging?"

He sat down on the curb, dropping his head into the palms of his hands. Jim stood by, nodding.

"If I only knew which way the wind's going to blow from now on," Jeff said, "I wouldn't have to squat here as blind as a pig in a poke. If that nigger-petition of hers catches on, I'd be a fool not to jump straddle the band-wagon. Nigger-trouble right now might be just the thing to set it off, too. People might begin falling all over themselves to get a chance to sign it to show their spite. I'd look like a pretty fool if I got left behind."

He looked up at Jim, almost convinced by his own reasoning.

"If a big politician like Senator Ashley Dukes plays safe, that's good reason why a sheriff ought to look out for his future, too." He watched Jim's face. "I feel I'm right, Jim."

"That sounds right," Jim said, "but you're down here between two fires. Senator Ashley Dukes don't have to run the risk of getting his fingers burnt up where he is. For all you know, that nigger-petition might back-fire and ruin everybody holding a political office in the county."

Jeff got up and put his hand on the car door. He glanced behind him at the second-story windows in the jailhouse to see if Corra had got up again. The windows were dark and silent.

"My wife's a wise woman, even if she ain't so much for looks," Jeff said, moving his head from side to side. "My wife told me to go fishing, and I reckon I'll just go ahead and do like she said. I'll be a lot better off down there sitting on a log across Lord's Creek than I'd be up here running myself frazzle-assed trying to find out something nobody is going to know the truth about till the shouting's over, anyway."

Jim watched him climb into his car and squeeze his belly under the steeringwheel. He was disappointed. He had hoped to induce the sheriff to change his mind so they could go out on a hunt for the Negro. The two joys of his life were hunting possums between midnight and dawn, and tracking down runaway Negroes at every opportunity.

Bert ran out of the jailhouse.

"There's another phone call coming in, Sheriff Jeff,"

he said excitedly. "I haven't answered it yet, because I thought you'd want to know about it if you hadn't left. What do you want me to do?"

"Go on and answer it," he answered quickly. "It's your job to take calls and promise nothing."

"Yes, sir," Bert said, turning around.

He had reached the screen door when Jeff called him. He came back to the porch steps.

"I'm going to listen to it, but that's all I'm going to do," he said, getting out of the car as quickly as he could. "Hold on, Bert."

Jim helped him squeeze his belly from under the wheel, and after that he was able to take care of himself. All three of them went inside.

They gathered around the phone. Bert lifted the receiver.

"Hello," Bert said. "Hello!"

"It had better not be Bob Watson again," Jeff said, eyeing the instrument suspiciously. "I'd be liable to lose my temper and tell him something this time."

"Hello!" Bert said again.

"Hello," the voice answered. "This is Avery Dennis." His voice was sharp and high-pitched with excitement. "This is Avery Dennis out at Flowery Branch. I want to report some trouble out here in the

33

neighborhood. There's a crowd of men out here in my corn field tramping down my crop. It's some of the crowd that's looking for that nigger, Sonny Clark. I don't care nothing about him, but them folks out there are ruining my field. I put a lot of work into my corn this year, all on my spare time, and I ain't going to stand and see it ruined."

"What do you want us to do?" Bert asked, turning and watching Jeff's face.

Jeff nodded tentatively. He was not certain that he approved of the question, but it was too late by then to do anything about it.

"Tell Sheriff McCurtain to come out here right away and drive them folks out of my corn field. He draws pay from the county for protecting property, and I want mine protected before it's too late. There ain't a nigger closer than a mile of here, noway. I'm going to get my shotgun and do some shooting of my own if them people ain't run out of my field. I don't have nothing against folks chasing niggers if they use care, but when they tramp down my corn field, drive automobiles over it, and ride mules through it, I just ain't going to be responsible for what happens to them. You tell Sheriff McCurtain I said all that."

"I wouldn't do anything rash, if I was you, Mr.

Dennis," Bert advised him. "It wouldn't pay you to get into trouble yourself."

Jeff looked worried. He leaned forward trying to hear what was being said.

"Then get Sheriff McCurtain out here to chase them off," Avery Dennis said. "That's what he got elected to office for, and he draws handsome pay the first of every month to do it. You tell him I said so."

"I'll see what can be done," Bert said, hanging the receiver on the hook.

"Who was that?" Jeff asked, his eyes jumping from the phone to Bert's face.

"Avery Dennis," Bert told him. "He says there's a crowd out at his place tramping down his crop of corn. He wants you to come out there and drive them out of the field."

Jeff sat down with relief. A faint smile spread over his face.

"I would have sworn it was some other damn fool wanting me to go catch that nigger before he gets lynched," he said. "It's nowhere like as bad as I thought it might be."

Bert and Jim waited in readiness, wondering if Jeff were going to send them out to Avery Dennis' farm instead of going himself.

Suddenly Jeff sat up erectly, sweeping the papers off his desk.

"Avery Dennis ain't got no business ringing me up on the phone at this time of night! Just look what time it is! Hot blast it, I might have been in bed sound asleep! Avery Dennis is a R.F.D. mail-carrier, anyway. Nobody on civil service has got a right to plague politicians who have to run for office ever so often! It's just them kind of people who always go nosing into politics. I've got troubles enough without taking on complaints from a frazzle-assed mail-carrier living on civil service. I ain't had no regard for people of that stripe since God-come-Wednesday."

He shook himself free of the chair and got to his feet. He looked larger than ever when he stood beside the small desk.

"Get me my fishing pole like I told you, Bert," he said brusquely, moving across the creaking floor.

"Yes, sir, Sheriff Jeff," Bert said, jumping. "I've got it standing against the wall on the front porch."

CHAPTER III

WHILE Sheriff Jeff McCurtain was getting into his automobile for the second time that night to drive down to Lord's Creek, Sonny Clark was creeping out of the deep piney woods that covered the whole southern slope of Earnshaw Ridge. Earnshaw Ridge was a long hump of red clay earth that protruded from the sandy flatlands and round hills of Julie County like a swollen artery. The hump began somewhere in the adjoining county to the west, ran angularly across the northern section of Julie County, and disappeared in a southeasterly direction in Smith County. At the foot of Earnshaw Ridge, Flowery Branch flowed in a meandering course southward through the lowlands towards the Oconee River.

Sonny had waded up the branch for about a mile and a half earlier in the evening and, after reaching the woods, he had lain trembling on the ground behind the fallen trunk of a dead tree for about two hours. Except for the two or three times he had been to Andrewjones, he had never in his life before been so far away from home. He had often wondered what was on the other side of Earnshaw Ridge, but for all he knew the world came to an end there and then.

He was creeping anxiously through the stiff underbrush at the edge of the woods. When he reached the clearing of an open field, he stopped and listened for a while. A hound was barking somewhere down in the lowlands, but there was no other sound in the night. He stood up and, after looking around in all directions, walked cautiously across the field in the direction of the plantation. He did not know any other place to go.

He moved across the field in spasms of haste, stopping abruptly when he thought he heard sounds, hurrying on again when the fear had passed. He knew unerringly the direction to take to the quarters where the Negro families lived on the plantation. He jumped a hedge and trotted joyfully in a furrow in a cultivated field. Each step that carried him closer home made him feel happier than he had ever felt before.

Sonny was eighteen years old and he lived with his grandmother, Mammy Taliaferro, in the Negro quarters on Bob Watson's plantation. He worked as a field-hand, and he earned enough money to support his grandmother and himself. Both of his parents had been killed about ten years before when a logging truck, running wild down Earnshaw Ridge, struck the wagon in which they were riding.

The cabins in the quarters rose up suddenly in front of him. The starlight made the fields, and even the buildings themselves, look as familiar in the night as they were during the day. He crouched in a ditch behind the first cabin for ten or fifteen minutes, because he wanted to feel sure it was safe for him to come out in the open so near the buildings.

He could not see anyone moving around the cabins, and there was not a light in any of them. It made him feel as lonely and afraid as he had been in the woods.

After a while he crept on his hands and knees to the back of the nearest cabin. Raising himself from his knees, he peered through a chink in the door.

By the rosy wavering flame of fat pine chunks he could see Henry Bagley and his wife, Vi, crouched over the hearth in the big room. Henry had always been Sonny's friend, and he had been thinking of Henry during the whole time he was hiding in the woods on Earnshaw Ridge. He was afraid to go to his own home. He knew he would have a hard time trying to explain to Mammy what had happened and, besides, he was afraid some white men might be waiting there to grab him the instant he showed his face.

Sonny waited breathlessly, his eyes fixed on the faint light from the hearth. It was several minutes before he could find enough courage to call Henry. Then he put his lips to the crack and breathed Henry's name.

Henry sat perfectly still. Only his eyes moved doorward.

"Who there?" he called in a low voice, startled and afraid.

Vi reached forward with as little movement as possible and threw another pine chunk on the fire. The room brightened.

"It's me, Henry," Sonny whispered. "It's Sonny."

"What you mean by whispering me out of my wits like that, boy?" he said. "Ain't you got no sense at all?"

"I didn't aim to scare you, Henry," he said.

Henry and Vi glanced at each other, each one nodding. Vi turned to see if the front door had the lock turned, and Henry got up and went cautiously to the back door. He put his ear against the door and listened to hear if he could detect sounds out there.

"Come on out here, Henry."

"What you want?"

"I got something to tell you."

Henry and Vi opened the door a few inches and looked out into the yard. Both of them saw him crouching on the ground in the corner between the doorstep and the side of the house.

Henry opened the door a little more and stepped down beside Sonny.

"What's the matter with you, boy?" he asked.

"I've gone and got myself into trouble, Henry," Sonny said, reaching up and clutching Henry's arm. "I done got myself into bad trouble, Henry."

"Boy, I got troubles of my own to worry about," Henry said.

"It's the worst trouble I ever been in in all my life, Henry. It just ain't ordinary trouble."

"What you been up to?"

"I ain't exactly been up to nothing myself," Sonny said. "It looks like trouble just came and grabbed hold of me, Henry."

"What you do?"

"I didn't mean to do it," Sonny said pleadingly. "I was just walking naturally along the big road about sundown last night, minding my own business as big

41

as you please, and then all at once something happened."

"What happened?" Henry urged, grasping Sonny's clutching hand. "Go on and say it, boy! What happened up there in the big road?"

"You know Mr. Shep Barlow, that white sharecropper of Mr. Bob's on the other side of the branch?"

"I knows him," Henry nodded. "I knows him good and well. What he done to you?"

"Mr. Shep himself didn't do nothing," Sonny said quickly. " 'Twas his girl. Miss Katy."

Vi vanished like a shadow into the cabin, noiselessly closing the door behind her. She stood on the inside whispering to Henry, trying to make him leave Sonny and come in where she was.

There was a long silence. Henry stared down into the upturned face of the crouching black boy. Sonny's face glistened in the starlight with running streams of perspiration.

"What was it, boy?" Henry demanded.

Sonny clutched at him with both hands.

"Miss Katy run out of the bushes and grabbed me and wouldn't let go," he said, trembling as he recalled what had happened. "Miss Katy wouldn't let go of me at all, and she kept on saying, 'I ain't going to tell nobody—I ain't going to tell nobody—I ain't going to tell nobody,' just like that. I said to her a colored boy didn't have no business standing there in the big road like that while she was around, but she wouldn't pay no heed to nothing I said. I don't know what got into her to make her carry-on like she done. She just kept on saying, 'I ain't going to tell nobody—I ain't going to tell nobody.' "

Henry tried to push Sonny's clutching hands away from him.

"Boy, you sure enough picked out the most trouble-some trouble there is when you done got yourself into this fix. Why didn't you haul off and get away from her? Why didn't you act like you had some little sense and run off? You ought to know better than standing still and listening to a white girl trying to get you in a fix. Where's your sense at, anyhow?"

Sonny got a tighter grip on Henry's arm.

"And that ain't all, neither, Henry," he said, his voice breaking and falling.

"Good Lord Almighty, boy! That ain't all! What you mean? Now don't tell me you ain't got a single spark of sense in that head of yours!"

"While I was standing there in the big road fidget-ing to make her leave hold of me, along come an automobile full of Mrs. Narcissa Calhoun, that white woman, and Preacher Felts. They jumped out and grabbed me right there where I was. I told them I was trying to get shed of Miss Katy, but they didn't pay me no mind. That white man pulled a knife, and I thought sure my time had come. He stomped me down on the ground and—"

"Boy," Henry breathed, grabbing him by the shoulder and shaking him roughly, "first you go and get yourself in trouble with a white girl—"

"Henry, I didn't go and do it! Miss Katy was the one who done it, because—"

"Makes no difference. You got yourself in trouble and then get caught by Mrs. Narcissa Calhoun. Don't you ever keep your ears open at all? That white woman is going all over the country getting up a paper to send all the colored to Africa or some place like that. And now you go and get yourself caught by her right when you and that white girl was standing—"

Sonny pulled at Henry, holding on to him with all his strength.

"I didn't have nothing to do with it, Henry," he pleaded. "I swear before the Good Lord, I didn't! It's that Miss Katy who's the cause of the trouble—"

"How come you squatting right here on the ground

44

at my back door like you is if Mrs. Narcissa and Preacher Felts caught you like you said they did?"

"They let me go."

"They did?" Henry said, amazed. "What made them go and do that-a-way?"

"Mrs. Narcissa said to let me go like I wanted to, because I wouldn't run off far, anyway."

Henry looked at him for a long time.

"Boy," he said at last, shaking his head from side to side, "you sure has gone and got yourself in a mess of trouble."

"What can I do now, Henry?" Sonny implored, moving closer.

"You'd better get yourself away from here, and be quick about it, too."

"But I didn't do nothing, Henry," Sonny protested. He began to sob. "I was walking along the road, coming home to supper from Mr. Bob's cornfield where I'd been chopping grass all day, and Miss Katy ran out of the bushes at me. I didn't never touch her none. She done all the touching there was her own self, Henry."

"Makes no difference with white folks, if touching was done," Henry said mournfully. "They ain't going to stop and figure like you and me. They going to step

45

out and do something big, and then figure afterwards. Don't you know Mrs. Narcissa Calhoun's going straight and tell the menfolks, and the sheriff, too, what she caught you at? The white folks ain't going to let a nigger be caught with a white girl, and then not do nothing about it. That Mrs. Narcissa wants her book full of names so she can have her way about sending the colored to Africa like she says. Makes no difference about nothing else with that white woman. I know what I'm talking about, boy."

Sonny crouched trembling on the ground, holding to Henry's hand as for dear life.

"Henry, I tell you I didn't do nothing to that white girl," he panted. He was on his knees by that time, clinging to Henry. Henry had begun to tug to free his hand from Sonny's grasp. "I ain't never touched a white girl in my whole life, and I never set out to neither. Miss Katy just run out and grabbed me her own self. She must have been hiding in the bushes I don't know how long, just waiting to run out like she done."

Henry struggled to free himself. He managed to move back against the door even though Sonny was hugging him around his knees.

"It don't make no difference at all what you say

you done, or not done," Henry told him with the calmness of despair, "because it's the white folks who's going to do the talking and acting, anyhow, from now on. They wouldn't stop to listen to nobody with a black face now."

"I don't know what to do," Sonny said desperately.

"I can tell you what to do. You get yourself away from here as fast as them legs of yours will carry you, that's what. And then keep on going after you get to where you thought you was going. Get yourself clean out of this country. You go straight north, and don't stop and fiddle around none till you get there, neither. This here country around Andrewjones ain't no place no more for a nigger caught fooling with a white girl."

"Where you mean, Henry?" Sonny begged, glancing fearfully over his shoulder. "Over on the other side of Earnshaw Ridge?"

"Boy, that ain't even the beginning of what I mean. I mean so far away on the other side you couldn't never see it again."

"I want to stay here and work the cotton and corn for Mr. Bob," Sonny whimpered. "I don't want to go nowhere a long way off. If they asked Miss Katy, she'd tell them I didn't have nothing to do with it—"

"Hush!" Henry whispered.

There was a sharp crunching sound that came from the direction of the road in front of the cabin. It sounded as if somebody had broken a dry shingle across his knee. A moment later several hounds began to bark.

Sonny crouched in the corner of the step. Henry tore his hand from the boy's frantic grip.

"What's that?" Sonny asked, his voice quivering.

Henry backed tighter against the door, feeling behind him for the latch.

Instead of saying anything, Henry shook his head, warning Sonny to be quiet. Then he reached down and touched the boy's head.

"On your way, boy," he told Sonny in a husky whisper. "This ain't no time to be hanging around my back door. There ain't no telling when the white folks will start swarming around here looking for you. They might be out there in the dark creeping up here right this minute."

Sonny threw both arms around Henry's legs. Henry could not shake him off.

"I don't want to go away from here, Henry," he said like a child lost in the dark. His eyes fastened on Henry's gleaming face. "I want to stay where Mammy is."

48

"Shut your mouth about Mammy. This ain't no time to be talking about Mammy. You went and let a low-down white girl get you into trouble, and now you got to get your own self out of it. First thing you know you'll have both me and Mammy in a mess ourselves. The white folks ain't going to stand for no butting in now, even if it was Mammy. Go on away from here like I done told you."

Sonny held him tighter.

"Will you tell Mammy for me that I didn't do nothing, Henry? Tell Mammy it wasn't none of my fault at all. Tell her it was Miss Katy who run out of the bushes and grabbed me. Will you tell Mammy that, Henry?"

"Sure," Henry said eagerly, pushing Sonny away from him. "I'll tell Mammy the first chance I get. Right now there ain't going to be no time to do nothing except hide out from them white folks on the hunt till they finish whatever they're going to do. Now, you go on off like I done told you already before. I'm getting scareder every minute I have to stand here like this."

Henry tore Sonny's arms from him and jumped back through the doorway. He slammed the door shut

49

and bolted it tightly on the inside, leaving Sonny clinging to the steps.

For a while Sonny crouched where he was, too frightened even to turn his head and look behind him. The moon still had not come up, but the starry night looked as if it had grown much brighter since midnight. When Sonny did find enough courage to turn his head and glance behind him, he could see the fence-rows crisscrossing the wide level land as plainly as he had seen them during the day when the sun was shining. Out across the fields he caught a glimpse of the persimmon trees jutting up like hands against the sky. He shut his eyes tightly, turning back again to look at Henry's cabin door. The cabin in which he himself lived with Mammy was almost out of sight, it was that far away, and he was afraid to move away from the shadow of the building where he was.

The dozen or more cabins in the quarters where Bob Watson's Negro field-hands and tenants lived were scattered along both sides of the lane for a distance of half a mile. There were still no lights visible in the quarters. Sonny beat on Henry's door with the flat of his hand, calling Henry. There was no answer. He crept on his hands and knees around the corner of the cabin and raised himself just high enough to put his eyes on the level of a crack under the tightly closed wooden shutter over the only window.

But Vi had already covered the pine chunks with ashes. He could not see even a gleam of light in the room.

"Henry!" he whispered through the crack.

There was no answer for a long time, even though he thought he heard Vi and Henry whispering to each other. The only other sound he could hear was the soft padding on the floor when Vi and Henry moved in their bare feet. They had taken off their shoes so as not to make any noise.

"Henry!" he whispered again, much louder than before. "Henry!"

"What you want now, boy?" Henry whispered back from the darkness of the room. His voice was not unkind, but it sounded as though he wished Sonny would go away.

"I just can't run off like you said, Henry," he pleaded. "I don't know how to go nowhere at all. I want to stay here. I ain't done nothing, Henry."

He could hear Vi and Henry whispering to each other, but he could not hear any of the words. He waited, hanging onto the window sill by his fingertips.

"If you ain't going 'way off like I told you," Henry said through the crack, "then just go off somewhere as far as you can from here and hide the best you can in the woods. But don't hang around here no longer, because the white folks is liable to come busting in here any minute from now on. You got sense enough to know they're going to get on the hunt. Go somewhere or other and find yourself a good place to hide, and just squat down and stay there. I'll come looking for you when the trouble dies down, if it ever does."

"You'll sure do that, Henry? You'll come and find me?"

"Ain't I always done like I promised?" Henry was pleading with him. "You strike out for the deep piney woods as fast as you can. Get going, boy, like I told you." His voice was urgent.

"All right, Henry," he said obediently. "I'm going just like you told me."

He dropped from the sill, feeling a lot better since Henry had told him he would not have to leave the plantation country. He could hide out in the woods near by any length of time as long as he knew he could come back when the trouble had died down and go back to work for Bob Watson in the cotton.

He tiptoed to the corner of the cabin and stood

52

listening with head bent a little on one side. The dogs had stopped barking and howling, and there was no sound anywhere that he could hear. Some crickets chirped near by, but they did not matter. He felt safe and comforted standing there at the corner of Henry's cabin.

All at once he was hungry. He remembered that he had missed his supper that night. He had never felt so hungry before in his life. If he went off into the woods as hungry as he was, and had to stay there several days, maybe a whole week, he knew he would starve. He turned around quickly on his heel and looked at the dark shuttered window. He called Henry's name several times, but there was no answer, He remembered that he had had only some cold turnip greens for dinner that day. He hugged his stomach with both arms, trying to ease the pain that had suddenly gripped him there.

He tried to pull the heavy wooden shutter open, but it was locked fast on the inside. Then he put his mouth against the only crack he could find and called Henry for a while, and then finally Vi. There was no answer.

Looking carefully in all directions first, Sonny crept

53

to the front door and tapped on it. There was no answer, and he knocked louder.

Henry came to the door and whispered.

"Who's that?"

"It's me, Henry," Sonny told him desperately. "It's Sonny."

There was a long period of silence.

"Why don't you go on off like I already told you?" Henry said harshly. "There's still time for you to go somewhere and hide out, boy."

"I'm hungry, Henry."

There was another interval of silence before Henry spoke again.

"Boy, you sure does hang on. I never saw the like of it before in all my life. You hang on and on, just like a new-born calf onto the old cow's teat. Ain't you got one drop of sense?" he asked impatiently, his voice rising.

"I'm hungry, Henry," he said meekly.

Henry and Vi whispered behind the door.

"I just can't go off to them woods hungry as I is. I ain't had a bite to eat at all."

"There won't be no need for you to eat," Henry warned him, "if you hang around here and let the white folks catch you. Dead people don't never have no craving to eat."

Sonny heard Henry's bare feet padding towards the kitchen, and he knew he was going to get something to eat after all. He crouched low at the door, turning his head just enough to enable him to watch the lane in both directions. All the cabins along the lane were as dark as the night itself. The whole settlement looked deserted. Sonny wondered as he crouched against the door if the people in the quarters, beside Henry and Vi, had heard anything yet. He decided they did know about his trouble, because he could think of no other reason why the cabins would be dark, even if it was after midnight, and the shutters closed over the windows on a hot summer night.

"Reach your hand through the crack when I open this door a little," Henry said, startling him. "Vi couldn't find nothing except some pieces of corn-bread, but that'll do you for a while. Now take what I'm giving you, and jerk your hand away fast, because I'm going to shut this door right up tight again. Next thing I know you'll be wanting to come in here and sleep in the bed. Do you hear me, boy?"

"I hear you, Henry," he said gratefully.

He put his hand on the door and waited for the

crack to appear. In a moment his hand slipped through the opening Henry had made, and he grasped the bread that was thrust at him. He began eating it in big mouthfuls right away.

"I ain't trying to be mean to you, boy," Henry said insistently. "I'm just trying to make you strike out for them deep woods where you belong. Now, get going! You hear me, boy?"

"I'm going, Henry," he promised. "I was just hungry."

He left the door, cramming the cornbread into his mouth and swallowing it in painful gulps. When he got to the back of the cabin, he stopped and listened, but there was nothing he could hear. He took one more look in the direction of the cabin where Mammy was, and then he crawled through the split-rail fence behind Henry's cabin and started walking across the field towards Earnshaw Ridge.

Halfway across the first field he suddenly remembered the rabbits. There was a persimmon tree not far away and, crouching, he ran to it. He pressed his body against the trunk of the tree. He thought he could almost see the rabbits half a mile away. They were in a hutch at the back of Mammy's chicken house.

He stood under the tree wondering if Mammy

56

would forget to feed them while he was away. She might forget, if she spent her time worrying about him, and they would be shut up with nothing to eat for two or three days, maybe a whole week, if he was away that long. The longer he gazed in the direction of the rabbits, the more troubled he became. Mammy was old and she forgot things easily. It hurt him to think of his rabbits shut up in the hutch and dying of starvation.

He made up his mind to go across the field to the back of the chicken house and feed the rabbits. He walked slowly across the field until he came to the ditch where the tall grass grew. He pulled up grass by the handful and stuffed it into his shirt. When he could not get any more into it, he ran along the side of the fence until he came to the rear of Mammy's cabin. The chicken house was only a few yards away. He could see the rabbits sitting in the starlight with their twitching noses poked through the mesh-wire. They began hopping around like mad when they saw him climb through the fence and come towards them.

Sonny stuffed the boxes full of the new green grass and put his hand inside to feel them. The two does sat where they were and let him rub their ears back and run his fingers through their fur. The buck was more cautious. He backed into a corner and stayed there eating grass with one ear raised and one flat on his neck.

"You sure like to eat, don't you, Jim Dandy?" he said to the buck, pushing a handful of grass closer. "You keep a man busy just feeding you and nothing else."

He had become so absorbed in the spell cast over him by his rabbits that he jumped when he remembered what it was he had to do. He looked around the corner of the chicken house towards the cabin, but the building was as dark as any of the others. He wished he could go inside and wake Mammy and tell her what had happened, but he remembered what Henry had told him, and he turned sadly away.

When he passed the box where the rabbits were, he stopped and looked inside again. Jim Dandy and the does were so busy eating the fresh grass that they had not moved in all that time. The box looked as if it were bursting with rabbits. All the young ones had started eating grass, too. They were hopping all over the place, nibbling first at one blade of grass, then hopping off to nibble at another one.

He was about to climb through the fence when he suddenly ran back and caught one of the little ones.

Holding it tightly in both hands, he climbed through the fence and ran out across the field.

When he came to a drain ditch where a patch of grass was growing, he stopped and snatched up several handfuls and stuffed it into his shirt. Then he put the rabbit in with the grass and buttoned the shirt carefully.

After that he ran across the field, not stopping until he reached the fence on the other side. When he stood up after climbing through, he could feel the rabbit's moist nose against his bare skin. It felt cool and friendly, and he was no longer lonely. He hurried along a path to Earnshaw Ridge, holding his elbows close to his sides so the motions of his body would not jolt and frighten the animal.

CHAPTER IV

A<small>FTER</small> leaving Andrewjones, Jeff McCurtain drove slowly down the highway through the low country, already missing his wife more than he thought he could endure for three or four days. He would find a Negro somewhere along the creek to cook his meals and keep him company, but even then he would be unhappy every minute. There was nothing in the world that could take the place of Corra's cooking and of her mere presence when night fell.

The highway was flat and straight, and he reached the narrow lane that led to Lord's Creek a lot quicker than he had wanted to. He slowed down the car, taking a last longing look at the low country before turning into the deep tangled swamp-growth that bordered the creek for two or three miles on each side of its banks.

The headlights of another automobile suddenly broke through the darkness and flashed upon him.

The car drew up behind him and jerked to a stop. He did not have time to move before he saw Jim Couch.

"I'm glad I caught you in time," Jim said breathlessly. "If you had got to the creek, I couldn't have found you till daylight."

"What in the world's the matter, Jim?" he asked.

"It's Judge Ben Allen, Sheriff Jeff," Jim replied quickly. "He said he wants to see you right away."

"Man alive, Jim!" Jeff exclaimed. "Why didn't you tell him I'd already gone to Lord's Creek? All he wanted was to know if I'd heard about the trouble and come down here, wasn't it?"

"I told him that, Sheriff Jeff," Jim said, watching his face, "and he said he wanted you to come back to town as fast as you could and come straight to see him."

Jeff dropped his hands from the steeringwheel. His wrists suddenly began throbbing with weakness.

"I don't know what far-fetched thing Judge Ben Allen could be thinking about," he said. "It ain't like him to change his mind and not want me to come down to the creek, after all these years."

"I don't know, either, Sheriff Jeff, but he sounded pretty positive talking on the phone."

Jeff gazed out at the fields of corn that covered the

61

land as far as he could see towards the east. On the other side of the road, the earth was alive with the tangled vegetation of the swamp. It looked peaceful and quiet out there towards the creek. The moon had come up, and the cool silvery light on the dew-drenched bushes reminded him of the night many years before when he walked seven miles to Corra's home to court her for the first time. He wondered why he was reminded of that night, and then he began wishing he could go back to the day they were married and start his life all over again. He knew if he could do that, he would avoid politics as if it were a plague.

"I'd sort of looked forward to a few days of peace and quiet down here on the creek, Jim," he said wearily. "It's about the only real pure vacation I ever have for myself."

"Maybe all Judge Ben Allen wants is to say a few words," Jim said sympathetically, "and you can come right back down here again."

Jeff looked at him hopefully.

"There is a chance of that, ain't there, Jim?"

"Sure," Jim told him. "The Judge wouldn't be likely to make any big changes. The primary election is a long way off."

"All right," Jeff said, speaking decisively. He started

the motor and began turning the car around. When he had got it straightened out, he called to Jim: "I'll hurry back to town and see Judge Ben Allen. You and Bert keep things like they should be at the jailhouse."

He drove off, working the car up into a high rate of speed immediately. He left Jim standing in the road.

It was eighteen miles back to Andrewjones, but he drove up the main street less than half an hour later. He passed through the courthouse square when it was only a few minutes past two o'clock and went directly up Maple Street towards Judge Ben Allen's house. On the way he passed the all-night filling station and saw three or four men standing beside a car while gasoline was being pumped into it. He speeded up so as not to be recognized. He was certain the men were getting ready to go to Flowery Branch and join in the hunt.

When he reached the driveway in front of Judge Ben Allen's house, he turned the car sharply and drove it under the wing of the building that had been built for the carriage entrance. He got out as quickly as he could, not even taking time to close the car-door.

He mounted the steps, crossed the porch, and began knocking vigorously on the paneling.

Judge Ben Allen had been a Circuit Court justice

63

for more than twenty years, and he had retired from the bench when he was sixty-five. His wife had been dead for eleven years, and he was alone in the world. If he had any close relatives, nobody in Andrewjones was aware of it, because he never mentioned the fact. The only visitors he had at his house were politicians. They invariably left after discussing the business that brought them there, and none of them had ever remained to pay a social call. Judge Ben Allen raised pigeons in his backyard. The house itself was the largest and whitest in Andrewjones. It was a three-story colonial with thick round columns that extended from the ground to the roof. The Democratic Party was split into two factions in Julie County, and Judge Ben Allen had taken over the leadership of the larger one. The Allen-Democrats had not lost an election since he had been in control, and the county was run by the politicians fortunate enough to be on friendly terms with him. The scarcity of Republican voters in the county had long before ruled out any possibility of a Republican running for an office, and the handful of people who otherwise would have voted that ticket were scattered among the two factions in the Democratic Party.

In a few minutes the door was opened by Wardlaw, Judge Ben Allen's Negro man. Wardlaw was several years younger than Judge Allen, but he looked almost twice as old. His hair was as white as cotton, and his body was bent. He walked in a shuffling manner with his body stooped.

Jeff pushed Wardlaw out of the way and went in, slamming the door behind him. Wardlaw got out of his way. It was not the first time the sheriff had come in a hurry to see the Judge.

Judge Ben Allen was waiting for Jeff in the library. He had on his nightgown and slippers, and Wardlaw had put a blue-and-white blanket around his shoulders. He was sitting at his desk.

"What's the matter, Judge?" Jeff asked at once, standing before him at the desk like a prisoner on trial.

Judge Allen looked up at him unsmilingly. Jeff could not recall ever having seen him before with such a worried expression on his face.

"You were a long time getting here to see me, McCurtain," he said. "I could have traveled that distance ten times over."

"I was down in the lower end of the county, near Lord's Creek, when I heard you wanted to see me."

"What were you doing down there at this time of

65

night?" he asked impatiently. "Why wasn't you in bed?"

Jeff looked at him carefully before answering. Judge Ben Allen had sent him fishing six or eight times during the past ten years, and he wondered if it were possible that the Judge was angry because for once he took it upon himself to go without being told.

"I was going fishing, Judge," he said finally.

Judge Ben Allen grunted and pulled the blanket tighter around his shoulders.

"This is a bad mess, McCurtain," he said gravely, speaking as though he were about to hand down an important decision from the bench. "Sit down, McCurtain."

Jeff sat down.

"This thing looks worse every minute," the Judge said, looking at Jeff and thinking. "That's the aggravating thing about it. We've got the primary elections coming along in less than four months. This is one time we've got to be sure of our ground."

Jeff nodded.

"Where have you been seen tonight since this thing got under way?"

"I was in bed asleep until a little after midnight," Jeff said quickly. "After that I got ready and got almost all the way to Lord's Creek. I ain't seen a soul tonight except my wife and the deputies."

Judge Allen looked at him, seemingly weighing the possibility that Jeff might be lying to him.

"We'll see," he said.

Wardlaw came in silently, sliding his wide flat feet noiselessly over the carpet. He went to the corner by the door and took up his accustomed position.

"I hate to say it about brother whites, Judge," Jeff began uneasily, "but them folks up there in those sand hills have got some far-fetched notions when it comes to mingling with niggers. I even found a white woman living with a nigger man up there once, but they ran off before I could do something about it. This Katy Barlow might be telling the truth, and, again, she might not be."

"There are more than a few bad actors with a hand in this thing, McCurtain," the Judge said, leaning back and pulling the blanket under his chin. "The one that's likely to cause me the most trouble is that Mrs. Narcissa Calhoun. This petition business of hers has come up so suddenly that no man alive can do any more at this point than guess what effect it is going to have on the election. The whole thing is blame foolishness from start to finish, but that won't keep it from causing trouble this near the election. People can be worked up to such a pitch over the rape of a white girl that they'll sign their names to any paper that comes along."

He stopped to think for a moment. After a while he turned and looked at Wardlaw standing in the corner.

"Wardlaw," he shouted, "I could send you to hell to burn in everlasting fire for your letting that nigger boy rape a white girl."

Wardlaw began to tremble.

"Please don't do that, Judge!" he begged. His lips began to tremble. "I won't never grumble over what you makes me do as long as I live!"

"That rape might set the opposition off on a clean sweep in the primary," he said, still looking at the Negro in the corner. "Say something! Don't just stand there shaking all the time!"

"I hope the opposition all goes to hell and burns in the everlasting fire," Wardlaw said, stumbling over the words. He was trying his best to remember what the Judge had said so he would be able to repeat it as he knew was expected of him. "I hope you'll send me to hell to burn in the everlasting fire because I let a nigger boy touch the white girl."

Judge Allen turned away from him.

"Don't you think I ought to hurry on down to the creek and start fishing right away, Judge?" Jeff asked hopefully. "If I left now, I could be there in half an hour."

"Fishing is something you ought to stay away from, McCurtain," the Judge said. "You ought to do something that'll give you exercise. Sitting on a creek fishing all day is the worst thing you could do. You wouldn't have to carry so much weight around if you took the proper exercise."

"I shed all my seasonal weight in the spring, Judge. I'm close to fifteen pounds lighter than I was last winter."

Judge Allen thought for a while, glancing casually around the room while he was making up his mind.

"I've decided you'd better get out there to Flowery Branch right away and make a show of trying to catch that nigger, McCurtain." He looked Jeff straight in the face. "That Calhoun woman is going to be out getting names on that petition of hers at the crack of dawn. If the people take to it the way I fear, it'll mean that we'll have to safeguard our interests by siding with the majority. I ain't in favor of sending the niggers to Africa, or anywhere else, no matter if every voter in Julie County signs the petition. But I can't let my personal feelings influence me at a time like this. We've got the courthouse full of our men who look to me to keep them in office. You're one of them, McCurtain. You want to stay in office, don't you?"

"Sure, I do, Judge, but—"

"Then get out there right away and move around in the act of trying to catch that nigger, at the same time dropping a hint that if you do catch him, he can be taken away from you if enough citizens demand that. By morning I'll have a chance to see how that petition is filling up. As soon as I know how to act, I'll send you the word."

Judge Ben Allen stood up. The blanket dropped to the floor.

"All of us have a big stake in county offices, McCurtain," he continued, "and we can't afford to let the opposition turn us out after all these years."

Jeff wished to suggest that it might be best if he went back to Lord's Creek and waited until the decision was reached, but he began thinking about the likelihood of his being defeated in the race for the sheriff's office, and he decided to do as Judge Ben Allen had told him.

It was difficult to imagine himself out of the sheriff's office after all those years of living on the top floor in the jailhouse. If he lost out there, he would have to take up farming. He did not know what else he could do for a living.

The phone on the desk rang, causing all three of them to jump. Wardlaw moved to answer it, but Judge Allen picked it up, motioning Wardlaw back to his corner.

"Is this Judge Ben Allen?" a woman's voice asked. He grunted affirmatively.

"Judge Allen, I'm awfully sorry to call you in the middle of the night like this, but I'm worried sick. I'm Mrs. Anderson out here at Flowery Branch. My husband has gone off with some other men to hunt for a nigger boy named Sonny Clark, and I'm afraid he'll be shot and killed by that nigger. I just know that nigger has a gun of some kind, and he might shoot my husband. Can't you do something? Has the sheriff gone out to capture him yet? Do you know what's happened since midnight? I'm out here all alone, and that nigger might break in the house and harm me. I think it's the sheriff's duty to track him down and kill him. When will that be done?"

Judge Allen nodded his head wearily at the phone.

"Maybe you'd better phone the sheriff's office, Mrs. Anderson," he said as calmly as he could. "The sheriff will help you. Good night."

He slammed the phone on the desk.

"Wardlaw!" he shouted. "If I ever catch you raping a white girl, I'll cut your gizzard out! Do you hear me!"

The old Negro jumped as if somebody had jabbed a pin into his flesh.

"Yes, sir, Judge, I heard you." He closed and opened his mouth several times. "If you ever catch me raping—" He wiggled his tongue in order to free himself of the words he knew he had to repeat. "If you ever catch me touching a white girl—" He paused again, choked with words. "If they ever catch me, they ought to cut the gizzard out of me."

He swayed unsteadily until he leaned back and placed his hands against the wall for support.

Jeff glanced uneasily at Judge Allen, his mind on the verge of urging him to try to persuade the Judge to let him go down to the creek at least until daylight. He had faith in Judge Allen's wisdom at a time like that, but he could not keep from remembering his wife's advice to stay away from Flowery Branch. If the crowd at Flowery Branch were given an opportunity to catch the Negro before he went out there, he would not be running the risk of making a lot of people switch their votes. His plurality in the last election was only one hundred and fifty-six votes. He was still waiting for an opportunity to suggest that he go down to the creek and stay at least until daylight when Judge Allen spoke.

"How many men can you deputize at this time of night, McCurtain?" he asked.

Jeff's heart sank.

"I hadn't given it any pure thought, Judge. It's hard to say, offhand. I reckon I could find a few, anyway. Maybe everybody's gone out to join the hunt, though."

Judge Allen walked from behind his desk, kicking the nightgown with his knees. He looked to Jeff like an old man getting ready to say his prayers.

"You'd better get busy and deputize as many men as you can lay your hands on," he said. His voice sounded measured and authoritative in the high-ceilinged room. "You ought to be out there within the next hour and see what you can do without taking action. Just as soon as I can determine which way we're going to jump, I'll send you word with the expectation that you'll act accordingly. In the light of a new day it may even appear wise for me to take steps to scotch

73

Mrs. Narcissa Calhoun's actions. I would see to it that the court issued a writ of *non compos mentis*. That would be effective in constraining her for some time to come." He started towards the door. "I'm glad I was able to catch you before you hid yourself down on that creek, McCurtain."

Jeff got to his feet, pushing his weight upward and balancing it on his legs.

"But, Judge," he said protestingly, unable to hold himself back any longer, "a deputized posse at a time like this might rub a lot of fur the wrong way. I've always believed in not going against the will of the common people. Besides, I want to see this lynching kept politically clean."

Judge Ben Allen stopped in the doorway and turned around for a moment.

"This lynching is going to be as clean as a cake of soap, McCurtain," he said. "I'm seeing to that."

The Judge turned and walked through the doorway, leading the way out of the room. When they reached the hall, Jeff went towards the door. Wardlaw held it open for him, closing it noisily after he had passed through it.

CHAPTER V

A LARGE crowd of men had collected in the Barlow front yard. Groups of them were milling around and around between the house and the barn, while some were standing in the fields surrounding the house in twos and threes. Most of the men were friends and neighbors who, like Shep himself, were tenants on Bob Watson's plantation.

The first ones to reach the house had started a smudge fire in the yard to keep the mosquitoes away. As time went on it began to look more and more like the beginning of one of the regular weekly possum hunts that nearly everybody in that part of the country took part in.

An automobile's headlights suddenly appeared in the lane a quarter of a mile away. Within a few moments word had spread through the crowd that it was Sheriff Jeff McCurtain coming to ask them to go home and let him capture Sonny Clark. Very little was said while they watched the car approach the house, but every man present was prepared to resist any effort to make them give up the hunt. Some of them muttered threats against the sheriff, but most of them waited grimly to see what was going to happen.

"Jeff McCurtain had better keep out of this," somebody said in a loud voice, each word a threat. "It just ain't healthy for him to come butting in around here now."

The crowd moved forward, surrounding the car when it came to a halt at the end of the lane. Several flashlights were turned on the car, and all the doors were jerked open. It was not the sheriff after all. The man who climbed out, blinking with fear in the dazzling light, was a barber named DeLoach from Andrewjones.

"What's the matter with you folks?" he managed to ask. He backed up against the car. "I ain't done nothing."

"What do you want out here?" somebody asked him, pushing through the crowd and standing before him.

"I heard about a nigger raping a white girl, and I wanted to help out in the hunt," he explained. "I've hunted down niggers before, and I didn't want to miss this one."

"He's all right," another man in the crowd said. "He cuts my hair in town once in a while. I've known him a long time."

The crowd drifted back into the yard, making the barber feel more comfortable. He followed the men to the smudge.

"Anything happened yet?" he asked.

Nobody said anything, but he could see some of the men shaking their heads.

"I was thinking only a few days ago that it was about time for something like this to happen again," the barber said. "The niggers have been laying low for about a whole year now, ever since that lynching down in Rimrod County. I was scared the next one was going to be off at the other end of the State, so far away I wouldn't have a chance to get there. But that's the way it is. If you figure back, you'll find out nigger-rapes take place just like clockwork. I've been keeping track of them ever since I started barbering in Andrewjones nine years ago."

Everyone seemed to agree with him, but nobody said anything. Most of the men around the smudge were farmers, and they had been neighbors of Shep's

77

almost all of their lives. There were only a few men from Andrewjones present, but because they were town dwellers they were looked upon as outsiders. The neighbors considered the trouble a personal matter, and they resented it when men from Andrewjones acted as though they had as much right to be there as anyone else.

"The last time I went on a nigger hunt was about three years ago," the barber said. "That was the time when we strung up that nigger down in Feeney County. He was a tough one to catch, believe me! It took us three days and nights to find him, because he'd hid in a swamp. That happened just about the same time of year it is right now, along about the middle of summer."

Before the barber from Andrewjones got there, the men had done a lot of talking about rape, but no one knew for certain what had actually happened. Even then, some of them were still skeptical. Two or three of the older men had not hesitated to say that it seemed strange that Mrs. Narcissa Calhoun, who everybody knew was promoting the Send-the-Negro-Back-to-Africa petition, was the only person who had said that Katy Barlow had been raped by Sonny Clark. So far even Katy herself had not opened her mouth about it, and a doctor had not been called in to examine her. The same handful of men were slow to believe that an eighteen-year-old Negro boy with a reputation as good as Sonny's would molest a white girl, even if it was Katy Barlow, unless he had received a lot of encouragement. One or two of them had come out openly and said the whole story sounded like something Mrs. Narcissa Calhoun had made up in a scheme to get signatures on her petition.

But most of the men were ready to believe anything against a Negro. One of them, Oscar Dent, operated a sawmill down in the Oconee swamp in the lower end of the county, and he had the reputation of fighting Negroes on every pretext he could find. Oscar had often boasted that he had killed so many Negroes that he had lost count. During the past winter he shot one to death at his lumber camp and killed another one with a crowbar. He had never been brought to trial for any of the killings, because he always claimed that he had acted in self-defense. After several unsuccessful attempts to indict him for manslaughter, the county prosecuting attorney had given up trying, because he said it only added to the expense of his office.

The excitement that had flared up when the barber from Andrewjones drove into the yard had died down. Voices were subdued. Many of the men were standing around the smudge, silently watching it smolder. Those who were talking were engaged in speculating about the price cotton would bring in the fall. If the price dropped under eight cents a pound, it meant that a lot of them would have to live on short rations for the next twelve months; but if the price went above ten cents a pound, they would not only be able to eat well, but also be able to buy some new clothes and a few pieces of new furniture. Day in and day out, the price of cotton was the most important thing in their lives.

Katy's father still had not returned home. Shep had driven off in a car shortly before midnight, and nobody knew where he was or when he was coming back. When he left, he said he did not want anything done until he got back and, since he was Katy's father, his wish had been respected. Everything connected with the preparation for the hunt depended upon Shep, and nothing could be done until he came back.

Katy was inside the house under the care of Mrs. Narcissa Calhoun. Narcissa had brought Katy home that evening, saying she was going to stay with her through the night. She planned to start out the next morning as soon as she had her breakfast and put in a full day obtaining signatures on the petition.

The smudge fire was smoldering briskly in the yard at the end of the path that led from the front door to the lane. The men had again scattered, and they were standing in small groups talking in low-pitched voices.

"You can bank on Shep Barlow," somebody standing beside the smudge said. "I don't know what he's up to now, but whatever it is, I'm with him. Maybe he knows where that nigger's hiding, and has gone to bring him in single-handed. That'd be just like Shep."

"I want to get started," another man said. "There ain't no sense in just standing around like this doing nothing. We could have that nigger caught by daylight if we'd go out after him."

"It's Shep's daughter that brought it all about," the other man said. "That being the case, I think it's only right to let him run it the way he wants it."

Shep had the reputation in Julie County of being the quickest-tempered man ever known. He never had confined his killings to the Negro race, because he acted without any delay when somebody made him angry. The last man he killed was a stranger, a white man nobody knew. The mystery of where he came from and where he was going, and even his name, had never been cleared up. Shep killed him for scarcely any reason at all. The stranger walked into the yard one morning about ten o'clock and drew himself a drink of water at the well without asking for it. Shep happened to be sitting on the porch, and he did not say a word. When the stranger was leaving, Shep walked out into the yard and slit the man's throat open with his pocketknife. The man lay there on the ground all afternoon and bled to death. At the inquest, the coroner asked Shep if he thought the man was deaf and dumb, and when Shep said he did not know one way or the other, the coroner said he was not going to hold a citizen to stand trial for murder just because he was an ignoramus. Shep said afterward that he did not like being called an ignoramus, but since both of them were Allen-Democrats, he was willing to forget it if the coroner would, too.

The light in the hall was turned on, and Katy came to the front door. She stood there for a while, peering out into the darkness. The men who saw her standing there recognized her at once. They moved closer to the porch where they could get a better view of her.

"I didn't know she'd growed up like that," a man whispered to somebody next to him. "She's a big girl now. I thought she was too young to look at a man."

"I've seen her around a lot of times the past year or so," the other man said, "but I never paid much notice of her. I always thought she was just one of the young ones."

"She might have been one of the young ones in the past," a man said as he moved towards the porch, "but she ain't no more. She's as bold as a bitch in heat. Just look at her up there!"

Katy's mother, Annie Barlow, had been dead for two years. Katy had just passed her thirteenth birthday at the time of her death. Her mother fell into the well one morning while she was drawing water to fill the washpot in the back yard. Shep had missed Annie that same evening when he came home for supper and found the meal had not been cooked and placed on the table at the proper time. He lost his temper and chased Katy out of the house, making her spend the night alone in the woods. Shep thought Annie had become peeved about something or other and had gone across the field to sulk a while, and that she would come back sometime during the night or early next morning in time to cook his breakfast for him. He was confident that when she did come back she would be as docile as ever. He went to bed that night and slept soundly. When he had to cook his own breakfast, he made up his mind to give her a good hard thrashing when she did come home. Late that afternoon she still had not returned, and Shep began to get a little worried. At dark he went over to Bob Watson's and got half a dozen Negroes to help him search the woods and fields near the house. They looked all that night and up to noon the next day, but not a trace of Annie was found. Shep finally sent word over to Smith County to find out if she had gone over there to stay with her father or sisters, but the word came back that she had not been seen there. Shep looked a little every day during the remainder of the week, and by Sunday he was ready to give up completely. He had finally decided that Annie had run off to Atlanta or Jacksonville or one of the other big cities. Late Sunday afternoon he was drawing a bucket of water at the well when the bucket struck something on the bottom he knew should not be there. He got Annie's hair-mirror from the house and ran back and cast a beam of light down into the well. He recognized Annie's red gingham dress the moment his eyes saw it. It made him much more angry to discover that Annie had been in the well all that time than he would have been if she had run away from home. He began shouting for Katy and throwing things into the well. Katy ran for the woods for fear he was going to throw her into the well as he was doing with everything else he could lay his hands on. There was nobody to stop him, and he kept on until most of the wood from the woodpile had been thrown down into it. Katy stayed away until the middle of the following week, but even then she was afraid to go to sleep at night during the rest of the summer while her father was digging a new well.

The men in the yard had crowded around the edge of the porch where they could get a better look at Katy. She smiled at the faces she could see clustered around the steps.

"Hi there, Katy!" somebody shouted excitedly.

She leaned forward, grinning at the men.

"Hi there, Katy!" the same voice shouted, louder than before.

Katy switched on the porch-light, turning the whole yard almost as bright as day. Most of the men who were leaning on the porch hastily backed away, but

85

others took their places, and before long nearly everyone was standing as close as he could get. Katy was still wearing the dress that had been ripped down the front from neck to hem. Mrs. Narcissa Calhoun had said that that was the way she found Katy, and that she wanted her to show what a Negro had done. Narcissa could be seen hovering behind the door, urging Katy to go out on the porch.

"Hi, Katy! How about it!" somebody called to her.

She opened the screen door and walked out on the porch. She stood where she was for several moments, turning her head every now and then when Narcissa said something to her. She looked as if she were embarrassed. Her face was flushed almost crimson.

Finally Narcissa stuck her face around the door and said something to her. Katy hesitated for a moment, and then she took several steps towards the edge of the porch. Almost everybody in the yard had begun to push and crowd around the porch. Katy crossed to the post by the steps.

"I could get my temper steamed up a lot hotter if it had been anybody else in the world that got raped," one of the older men in the rear said.

"Katy Barlow ain't got exactly the best reputation I've heard about," another one said, "but it ain't exactly her fault. Her old man just ain't taken proper care of her since the girl's mother was found dead."

"That's true enough," the other one said, "but I just can't seem to be able to work up a temper over it."

Katy was smiling down at the faces glowing in the light. She put one arm around the post, supporting herself, and fingered the torn opening in her dress. The crowd surged forward in an effort to get a closer view of her when she moved the opening in the garment.

"Hi there, Katy! How about me!"

She smiled broadly at the faces, her face burning with excitement.

Several men who had been standing at the edge of the porch directly under her, pushed their way out of the crowd and backed off to the smudge. DeLoach, the barber from Andrewjones, worked his way through the closely packed crowd. They gathered around the smoking smudge fire, watching Katy. Nobody said anything for several minutes.

Milo Scoggins, a tenant farmer who lived about two miles down the road, came up where DeLoach and the others were standing. He took a bottle of corn liquor from his pocket and passed it around. After the others had had a drink, he turned it up and finished it.

"I ain't seen anybody tonight who knows anything about her," the barber said, jerking his head in the direction of Katy on the porch. "It's funny that she's been living around here all this time and nobody's ever had anything to do with her."

"You ain't been asking the right folks," Milo said. "You ain't ask me nothing about her."

All of them crowded around Milo. The barber nudged him with his elbow.

"Have you ever noticed her doing anything?" De-Loach asked quickly, nudging him again and again.

"Noticed her?" Milo said, smiling.

DeLoach nodded several times, still nudging him in the ribs.

"Last fall I was picking cotton for Bob Watson, over in a field about three and a half miles from here," Milo said. "Bob Watson owns all the land in this part of the country, and nearly everybody around here works for him, renting or sharecropping or something. There was about thirty-five or forty of us in his field picking cotton this time I'm talking about."

"What about her?" the barber asked impatiently, jerking his head towards Katy.

"Hold your patience," Milo said, pushing him away. "I'm coming to that part. We was all picking cotton, and Katy Barlow was, too. I noticed all morning that she kept edging up to the boys, and so that afternoon about three o'clock I decided I was going to find out what she was up to. I fell behind the rest of the pickers a little, and it wasn't long before she dropped behind, too. I talked to her some, trying to feel her out, and she appeared to be just as willing as they ever get. Right then I out and asked her how about meeting me when the picking-day was over, and she said she would."

He paused and looked around to see if anyone else had come up to the smudge. The other men looked at Katy on the porch while they were waiting for Milo to continue. DeLoach pranched around excitedly, nudging him.

"A little before sundown, when the pickers was leaving the field to go home, I made a sign at Katy, and she followed me to the fieldhouse where we had been dumping our pickings all day. I crawled inside and waited, watching her through a crack in the wall as she came across the field. Pretty soon she came jumping in and climbed over the cotton to where I was. I never saw a girl so man-crazy before in all my life. In no time at all she had stripped herself down to her bare skin. I'm here to tell you I never saw a prettier sight than I saw then. She stretched out on the cotton, all naked and soft-looking. Where her legs came together at her belly it looked exactly like somebody had poked his finger in one of these toy balloons, and the place had stayed there. She—"

There was a commotion in the crowd around the step. Milo stopped and turned around to see what was happening. Katy was laughing nervously and pulling the dress together where it had fallen open.

"Hi there, Katy! Don't forget me!" somebody shouted above the uproar.

DeLoach, the barber, again began nudging Milo in his ribs. Milo jumped every time the barber's sharp elbow jabbed him.

"What did you do then?" the barber urged.

One of the other men took out a bottle and passed it around. They drank it empty and tossed it aside.

"I didn't do nothing then, to tell the truth," Milo said, wiping his mouth with the back of his hand. "She lay there carrying on with herself like I never saw before in all my life. Then the next thing I knew she had started in on me the same way. We started rolling around getting at each other. That fieldhouse of Bob Watson's is about thirty or forty feet square on all sides, and one time we would be bumping up against the side of one wall, and the next time against the other wall, that far away. She got hold of me with her teeth, and I thought she was going to kill me, it hurt so much. I yelled loud enough to be heard a mile away. I reckon I must have lost my head, because I started beating her with my fists, the pain was so bad. It looked like she didn't mind that at all, because right away she started making a sound like pigeons cooing. Her teeth-bites didn't hurt as much after that, and all I could hear was that pigeon-cooing sound. That lasted I don't know how long, but the next thing I knew we was rolling again, all over the cotton. We smashed into a wall, knocking me silly as a jaybird. I didn't care. What brought me to, was her getting a fresh grip on me with her teeth. I tried to beat her off with my fists, but she wouldn't let go no matter how hard I hit her. The next thing I remember was when I opened my eyes and saw blood smeared all over both of us. Them sharp teeth of hers had took a bite out of my shoulder the last time, and I've got the scar right this minute to show for it. I reckon that scar will be there on me for the rest of my life."

There was nothing said after he had finished. De-Loach, the barber, stood staring at him. After a while he walked off into the darkness towards the barn.

Milo and the other men moved towards the crowd around the porch step.

"Hi, Katy!" somebody shouted at her.

Milo pushed forward and took a good look at her.

"She's got that same look on her," he said, whispering to one of the men who had followed him from the smudge. "That's exactly the way she looked that time in Bob Watson's fieldhouse."

Moths were fluttering around the light bulb on the porch ceiling, many of them flying against her face. She raised her hand and brushed some of them away. When her dress fell open, she pulled the ends together, giggling.

"Hi, Katy!" a voice, deeper than any of the others, shouted from the darkness of the yard.

She giggled so much she had to clutch the post with both arms in order to support herself.

CHAPTER VI

AFTER leaving Judge Ben Allen's door, Jeff McCurtain got into his car heavy-heartedly, and drove back downtown. Passing as quickly as possible the all-night filling station, which was now dark and deserted, he rode slowly around the Julie County courthouse time after time. His mind was tormented by the urge to follow Judge Allen's advice for the sake of his political future, but it was his own conviction that more harm than good would come from any interference with a hunt-hungry crowd of men bent on lynching a Negro. He knew from past experience that Judge Allen was playing the situation as he would a game of checkers, and that whenever the opportunity presented itself, Judge Allen would gladly sacrifice one man in order to jump two. Jeff lamented the fact that the threatened law-breaking was not something out-and-out one-sided, such as common breaking-and-entry, or bail-jumping.

He did not know how many times he had circled the tall, spire-topped, red-brick building, but he had gone around and around so often that he began to feel dizzy. He felt the car zigzagging in the street, but he had enough presence of mind to bring it to a stop. He looked out and recognized the east side of the courthouse square.

He was wondering who Judge Allen would choose to succeed him in office if the people turned against him when he suddenly felt deathly sick in his stomach. He slumped over the steeringwheel.

When he opened his eyes and sat up, he did not know how long he had been there, but he felt much better. He tried to find the illuminated clock-face on the courthouse tower, but the heavy foliage on the trees hid it from view.

Jeff had no idea where the idea came from, but from somewhere in his dazed mind had come the thought that it would be possible for him to keep from getting involved politically in the trouble at Flowery Branch. He remembered that while he was circling the square he had wished he could go somewhere and get the remainder of his night's sleep. Now he had a plan that would enable him to do both.

"Man alive!" he said to himself, getting out of the

94

car and stretching his legs. "I'd have worked myself lop-sided out there at a time like this."

He felt a lot better already. He was confident that, instead of losing votes in the coming primaries, he would invoke so much sympathy from the people that he would get more votes this time than he had ever before received.

Jeff walked up and down beside the car several times, limbering his muscles. He had been so thoroughly carried away by his enthusiasm that he had forgotten where he was. He ducked into the shadow of the car and looked around to make certain no one was observing him. He had happened to think that if the night town patrolman had been on the job, he would not have escaped being seen in the middle of the square at that hour. Seeing no one, he started down the street wondering if the patrolman had left town and gone to Flowery Branch.

Walking hurriedly, and yet being careful not to let his heels click and scrape on the concrete sidewalk, he went in the direction of the rear end of the jailhouse. He went three blocks out of his way in order to avoid being seen by chance anywhere near the front part of the building.

It made him feel good all over to think how, almost

accidentally, he had found a way to satisfy everybody, politically speaking, including both Judge Ben Allen and himself. He thought his plan such a good one that even Corra would be pleased when she heard about it. He walked as fast as he could, swinging the weight of his body forward with a nimbleness that he once thought was gone forever.

At the rear of the jailhouse he stopped and listened. It was as quiet as a tomb in a country graveyard. The street lights flickered through the trees, making patterns on the pavement that reminded him of his wife's fancy needlework.

Going carefully to the rear door, he took out his ring of keys and searched for the proper one. The key opened the lock, making only a single rusty squeak. He listened for a moment and then, secure in the knowledge that the noise had not attracted attention, he opened the door and stepped inside. He was careful to leave the door wide open.

Jeff stood in the darkness of the cage-room listening to the sound of Sam Brinson's heavy breathing. Sam's presence seemed to make everything all right from that moment on.

He felt his way through the passage between the two tiers of cages. It was pitch black in the room and he had to feel every inch of his way along the passage.

It was no trouble to feel the familiar pass-key on the ring, and he unlocked one of the cages and let himself inside. The rusty hinges creaked loudly when he moved the steel-barred door, but Sam Brinson's heavy breathing continued without a pause. He had selected one of the cages on the south side of the passageway, because he remembered distinctly having locked Sam in the colored man's usual cage on the opposite side.

Jeff closed the door slowly, taking care not to allow it to squeak any more than necessary. When it was closed, he put his hand between the bars, locked it, and tossed the ring of keys down the passageway as far as he could heave them.

He knew precisely what he was going to tell Bert the next morning when Bert came to give Sam Brinson his breakfast. He was going to explain that he was in the act of carrying out Judge Ben Allen's orders when five men, masked with handkerchiefs tied over their faces, had abducted him in the courthouse square, threatening to knock him unconscious with pistol-butts if he made any outcry. After they had taken his keys from him, they locked him in the jailhouse, threw the keys away, and left before he could call for help.

He planned to tell Judge Ben Allen that the men had locked him up in his own jailhouse and told him they were doing it in order to keep him from organizing a posse and interfering with their search for Sonny Clark. Judge Allen would not be able to hold him responsible for failing to deputize a posse as he had ordered and, what was equally as important, he would not have to go out to Flowery Branch and commit political suicide by antagonizing voters who were determined to catch the Negro.

Jeff chuckled to himself, his flesh shaking pleasantly, when he thought how lucky he was to have been able to think of such a fool-proof scheme. He knew Corra would be pleased, too, when she found out how well he had taken care of his political interests. She would be sure to forgive him for his failure to hide himself on Lord's Creek.

"Man alive!" he whispered to himself. "If I had gone out there to Flowery Branch, it would have been just like cutting my own throat. That would have been a foolish, far-fetched thing for me to do."

He felt sorry for the little Negro boy, Sonny Clark. A feeling of helplessness came over him. He hated to think of the boy's life being taken away from him, but now that the situation was threatening his own political existence he knew he would have to safeguard his future at any cost. He tried to put Sonny out of his mind by thinking how sleepy he was.

There were two tiers of bunks in the cage, each tier containing two sleeping-shelves. Jeff felt his way to the bottom bunk on the left. He searched through his pockets for matches, but could not find a single one. He sat down anyway, and took off his shoes. In a few moments he was stretched out on his back sound asleep.

During the night he woke up once when he thought he heard several men shouting somewhere about the jailhouse, but he could not keep awake long enough to open his eyes. He turned over with his face against the wall and went back to sleep.

Just as dawn was breaking, shouting voices again woke him up. He awoke with a start. Before he could turn over, the high-ceilinged room was filled with sound. Some of the voices were raised to a high pitch. He was certain one of them was Corra's.

He turned over quickly in spite of his weight and bulk and put his feet on the floor.

"What's the matter!" he shouted, trying to see between the bars.

When his eyes swept the cage, he had the distinct

feeling that everything was not as it should have been. He turned away from the door and looked at the opposite bunk. He sat up so erectly that he cracked his head on the steel frame of the bunk above. A Mulatto girl was lying on the bunk in front of him. She sat up suddenly and screamed at the top of her voice.

Jeff rubbed his eyes unbelievingly.

Just then there was a quick rush of heavy footsteps in the passageway.

"Man alive!" he yelled. "Where am I?"

He turned and looked through the barred door. He could see several strange-appearing faces straining to get a glimpse of him. After a moment he realized that the faces on the other side of the door were covered with handkerchiefs, and he had the fearful feeling of being in a dream and not being able to wake up from it. The masked faces looked exactly like the ones he had imagined so clearly when he was locking himself in the cage. Behind them all he could see dimly the familiar features of Corra, Bert, and Jim Couch.

"Corra!" he shouted as loud as he could.

The Mulatto girl sat wild-eyed before him, pulling her disarrayed clothes around her. In another moment she was again filling the cage with ear-splitting screams.

"Great God, Corra!" he shouted, jumping to his

feet and rushing to the door. "Get me out of here!"

The handkerchief-masked men crowded around the door, shutting Corra from sight.

"Where's that Clark nigger, Sheriff?" one of them said calmly.

He could see several gun-barrels pointing between the bars at him. He stepped backward a little.

Corra pushed between the men and stood facing him a few feet away. She was gazing at him coldly.

"What are you doing, Jefferson?" she asked sharply. The instant he heard her voice he knew he was no longer floundering in a dream. "Jefferson!" she said.

"Corra, I didn't—"

He glanced at the Mulatto girl from the corners of his eyes.

"Now, look here, Sheriff," one of the men said gruffly, "we ain't got time to waste on drivel-dravel. We—"

"I'm Jeff McCurtain! Nobody can order—"

Several gun-points were shoved through the bars, prodding him painfully in the stomach.

"We want to know what you done with that Clark nigger," the gruff voice rose in his ears. "Word got around that you'd caught him and brought him to town and locked him up in the jailhouse. We ain't got no time to lose. Where's that Clark nigger, Sheriff?"

"I don't know who none of you is," Jeff said, rising up, "but nobody's going to come in my jailhouse and scare the wits out of me. I got elected to this office, and I've been re-elected time after time to it, and I'm going to run it my own way as long as I get the votes to keep me here."

"You'd better get out and start fixing your fences then, McCurtain," another voice said. "When the people hear about this, they're going to start stampeding for greener pastures."

"Where's that nigger at, Sheriff?" the other voice said impatiently.

"Boys, I ain't seen nothing of Sonny Clark," Jeff said quickly. "I hate like all get-out to be seen here like this, but it was all a pure accident. If you folks will just hold on a minute—"

"Nobody cares about that, McCurtain," one of the other men said. "We want that nigger."

Corra was standing directly in front of him by then. She was gazing at him as though she had never seen him before in her life.

"If you know what's good for you, Sheriff, you'll quit stalling and turn that Clark nigger over to us."

"What's that nigger girl doing in there with you, Jefferson?" Corra spoke up.

"Who, her?" Jeff asked, turning and pointing at the girl on the bunk.

"Why didn't you go off fishing like I told you?" she said, ignoring his motions.

Jeff opened his mouth to protest, but one of the masked men shoved a shotgun against his chest.

"We ain't got time to stand here and listen to you and your wife squabble, McCurtain," a man said roughly. He turned to Corra. "I'm sorry we got to be so short with you, Mrs. McCurtain, but we ain't got no time to lose." He turned back and faced Jeff. "We want that Clark nigger, and we want him quick. You and your missus can finish your squabbling when we get through."

"Boys, I don't know nothing in the world about—"

"Come on, McCurtain! Quit your stalling!"

Jeff turned and looked helplessly at the girl. She had drawn herself into the far corner of the bunk and was staring at the guns.

"Boys, I swear I ain't seen Sonny Clark," Jeff said earnestly. "I wouldn't lie, boys. I got my political future to think about. That's why I couldn't lie about it. You folks know me better than to think that, don't you?"

"This ain't no time to be asking us questions, Mc-Curtain. We're doing that part ourselves."

Jeff tried to look between the bars and see why Bert and Jim did not take some action when the jailhouse was being held up like that. He saw that both of them had guns shoved against their sides.

"Boys," Jeff pleaded, "everybody in Julie County knows I'm a man of my word. I've been running on that plank ever since I went into politics. The common people have voted me into office ever time I've been up for re-election just on that account. You can believe—"

"You can have that put on your tombstone, Mc-Curtain," one of the men said roughly. "Right now all we care about is getting that nigger you're hiding somewhere."

The two men guarding Bert and Jim pushed them down the passageway, flashlighting each cage as they went along. Two of the men stayed to guard Jeff, and the fifth one watched Corra.

"Jefferson!" Corra said, her eyes not leaving his face for an instant. "The idea of you laying-up with a nigger girl right here in the jailhouse! I've got a good mind to walk off and leave you for good and all!"

"Mrs. McCurtain," the man behind her said, "you'd better stay right where you is. We won't be long now."

"Corra," Jeff pleaded, "I don't know nothing about how she came to be in this cage where I am." He turned and surveyed the girl timorously. "I was only trying to keep the lynching clean politically. I didn't know—"

The other men came back, pushing Bert and Jim along as though they had been convicted prisoners themselves.

"Where'd you hide that nigger, McCurtain?" one of the men demanded. "It ain't as long as you think till election-time. Is it, Mrs. McCurtain?"

Corra clamped her lips into a thin straight line.

"Julie County ain't never had much regard for a nigger-loving sheriff, now has it, Mrs. McCurtain?" the man asked, turning and looking at Jeff.

Corra ignored the question.

Jeff shook his head, moving it from side to side so that all might see. He could not keep from observing Bert's and Jim's inquisitive looks, but what worried him most was his wife's scandalized stare.

"Boys," he began hopefully, "I was on my way to

go fishing down at Lord's Creek when all this trouble started." He paused and looked from face to face, feeling weary with discouragement when the handkerchief-masked men did not respond to his story. He took a firmer grip around the bars. "I did go up to see Judge Ben Allen, but I ended up right here where you see me now. I ain't been within ten miles of that Clark nigger, that I know of. I don't know no more about him than the next one to come along."

The men were silent. While he watched their expressionless faces, he hoped that nobody would think to ask him then how he came to be locked up in his own jailhouse, and in the same cage with a colored girl, at that.

"You heard what the man said, Corra," he urged. "You can tell him I'm saying only what's what."

Corra pretended to ignore him completely.

"Boys," he said, turning to the men around the door once more, "I give you my word as sheriff of Julie County that I ain't got the slightest notion where that Sonny Clark's at. That's the pure truth if I ever told it."

Two of the men withdrew from sight. The dawn was turning the inside of the room into a dull, dirty gray. Jeff could hear the men whispering in low voices.

He was not worried at first, but later he began to fear that they might be discussing whether they wanted to take him along with them. He looked imploringly at his wife, hoping for help from her.

The two men came back, demanding the jail keys from Bert. Bert handed them over without protest. The men unlocked the door to Sam Brinson's cage and prodded him with a gun. Sam came tumbling out into the passageway, shaken with fright.

"Now, hold on there!" Jeff said, realizing what was taking place. "Sam Brinson ain't done no harm to nobody."

"We'll just take him along in case that other one don't turn up," a man said over his shoulder.

Sam shook from head to heel, blinking in the early morning light.

"Stand up there, nigger!" he was ordered.

"White folks, please, sir, I ain't done no wrong!" Sam said. "I declare to goodness, I ain't. You just ask Mr. Jeff about me, please, sir. Mr. Jeff'll tell you about me!"

"Shut up, nigger!"

"Hold on there!" Jeff spoke up. "I wouldn't go against the will of the people if they want to catch that Clark nigger, but I'll stand up for Sam Brinson any day. Sam ain't never done anybody harm in all his life, and I ain't going to let nothing happen to him."

"What's he doing in jail, then?" the man said.

"It's just temporary this time," Jeff said at once. "They promised me over at the courthouse they'd nol-pros the charges against him and enter a writ of replevin instead. Sam's always trading and swapping old cars. Sometimes when he gets into a deal over his head, I just lock him up for a while."

"That legal talk don't make sense to me."

"White folks," Sam said beseechingly, "if you all will let me go this time, I won't never trade machines again. I'll shut my eyes every time I see a machine looking my way."

"Shut up, nigger!" one of the men said, jabbing him in the ribs with a rifle. "Your mouth's too big for the size of your face. It don't look becoming when you open it."

"Sam Brinson ain't done a thing to be harmed about," Jeff insisted, raising his voice. "He was only locked up this time because he traded a worn-out old bicycle he picked up down on the town dump for a wrecked car that wasn't worth no more than it's weight in scrap iron. There wouldn't been no harm in that, except he mortgaged it for three dollars in cash, and then turned around and swapped it for another old machine that wouldn't even roll when you push it. It just happened that he didn't get the old car mortgage-free before sundown because he turned around and bought back the bicycle for three dollars. The man wouldn't take in the old bicycle to clear the mortgage, and the three dollars cash was gone, so that's why he got in a fix this time. If sundown had only held off half an hour longer, Sam would've been as clean-handed as the folks who run the bank."

The men did not say anything right away. They looked at each other, trying to figure out the trail of involved deals Sam had made.

"Everybody knows Sam Brinston is just a fool about old automobiles, like a lot of Geechee niggers is," Jeff spoke up. "He ain't like the common breed of field-hand bucks. Sam's been swapping and trading old worn-out rattletraps ever since God-come-Wednesday. Last month the grand jury threatened to return a true bill against him if he didn't stop signing fraudulent conveyances when he made his swaps, but I don't hold that against him. Brother whites make missteps, too, if they ain't acquainted with the law."

"Shut up, McCurtain," the tall man said, coming

to the door. "You figure out them deals your own self. A white girl's been tampered with, and the niggers has got to suffer for it."

They began poking Sam down the passageway.

"But nobody ought to harm poor old Sam Brinson when he don't know no more about it than I do! Sam couldn't have done it! He's been locked up here in the jailhouse since two days before the trouble started!"

"You get busy and hand over that other one if you want this one back, McCurtain," he stated. "And if you ain't going to, you'd better save your talk for electioneering. It's just before votes is counted when you'll need talking the most."

All the men backed down the passageway.

"Don't nobody move out of their tracks for five minutes," one of them shouted back. "And don't nobody make a move to follow us. There'll be plenty of shooting if anybody does!"

Jeff sank down on the bunk, limp with worry. The first thing he saw was the figure of the yellow-skinned girl drawn up before his eyes. He dropped his gaze, staring blankly at the soiled concrete floor.

Corra moved silently up to the barred door.

"What have you got to say about all this?" she demanded.

He shook his head from side to side.

"I've never felt so frazzle-assed before in all my born days," he said weakly.

Bert and Jim moved up to the bars and looked at him sitting dejectedly on the side of the bunk.

"Get some keys and open this door, Bert!" he ordered meanly, looking up. "Don't just stand there and gape at me like a blame fool!"

"Yes, sir, Sheriff Jeff," Bert said, moving quickly.

He unlocked the door with the key from his own ring. The door swung open noisily, squeaking on all four rusty hinges.

The girl sat up.

"Is you the real sheriff, sure enough?" she asked boldly. "I thought you looked like Sheriff McCurtain, but I didn't see how come the real sheriff would be locked up in the jailhouse."

Jeff glared at her.

"Oh, Lordy me!" she cried, pushing herself into the corner.

Jeff got up, put on his shoes, and slid the soles over the rough concrete, moving himself in the direction of the door. Bert and Jim stepped aside as he walked haltingly between them. He looked like a man who had been through a great ordeal within a short period of time.

"Bert," he said, "who put that nigger girl in this jailhouse?"

Bert did not answer immediately. He looked down at the floor.

Jeff looked at Jim Couch. Jim's face was solemn.

"How long has she been in here?"

"About two days, I think, Sheriff Jeff," Jim answered, looking away.

"Who put her in?"

Both Bert and Jim looked as if a great weight were falling upon their backs.

"Somebody is going to tell me. The county pays you deputies a good salary to answer my questions when I ask them, don't it?"

Jim looked him straight in the face, nodding.

"I put her in, Sheriff Jeff," he said meekly. "It was me."

"Turn her out," Jeff ordered. "And be quick about it."

Bert and Jim went into the cage and motioned to the girl to get up and leave. She ran through the rear door as fast as she could.

"I've told you deputies I wanted that stopped," he said, glaring at them. He turned and walked painfully towards the door that led to his office in the front of the building. "If I ever catch another nigger girl in my jailhouse, I'll fire both of you."

He had taken two or three steps when he felt the stinging crash of a human palm against his face. He had forgotten all about Corra momentarily. Before he could guard against it, he felt the blistering impact of two more painful slaps on the other side of his face. He threw up his arms protectingly.

Bert and Jim cowered in the corner.

"You've got a lot to answer for, Jefferson McCurtain!" Corra said coldly. She raised her hand again as if to strike him another time, but he lowered his head into the protecting cover of his arms. "I never thought you'd disgrace me right in my own home! How can I walk along the streets of Andrewjones and hold my head up after this?"

He looked at her through the protection of his raised arms. She was regarding him angrily.

"Honey," he said appealingly, "I didn't know she was in that cage until I woke up just a while ago. And, besides, you know I ain't touched a colored girl since that last time. You ought to believe me, honey."

"I don't believe that when I can see as plain as day with my own eyes!"

Bert and Jim tiptoed noiselessly through the door into the office. They closed the door carefully.

"Why did you deceive me by trying to make me believe you was going fishing at Lord's Creek, and then slip back here with a nigger girl? Answer me!"

"Judge Ben Allen—"

"Trying to put the blame on that old man!" she said disdainfully.

"Honey, he told me not to go fishing because he was worried about Mrs. Narcissa Calhoun's petition and said I ought to go out and catch that nigger boy before—"

"You'll be one that'll never sign that petition, Jefferson McCurtain, because you don't want the nigger girls to be sent out of the country!"

"Honey, that ain't so! I'll sign it right now and show you!" He looked at her hopefully, taking several steps towards her. "Honey, I was afraid to do what Judge Ben Allen said do, because I was afraid of the political risk if I showed my face at Flowery Branch. I was doing my best to keep this lynching politically clean. That's how come I locked myself up in here and was going to say—"

He paused and attempted to measure the degree of his success. Corra stared back at him.

"Honey, I done what I done and was going to tell Judge Ben Allen and the people that some unknown men with handkerchiefs tied over their faces took me out of my car and locked me up so I couldn't interfere with them catching that nigger boy. That's the pure truth, honey."

He paused, panting.

"Go on!" Corra said, stepping back from him.

"That's all, honey. But it didn't work out because them other men showed up just a while ago and spoiled everything I had all planned out in advance."

"If that's part of your cock-and-bull story, what's the rest of it? I may as well listen to all of it while I'm about it, because I won't be staying under this roof long enough to hear it after I walk away from here."

"I crept in in the dark, honey," he began desperately, fighting for breath to enable him to tell it as quickly as possible, "and then I locked myself up in that cage without knowing anybody in the world was in it. I didn't know that until just a while ago when I woke up." He stopped and looked around for Bert and Jim. "You heard them deputies say they locked her up in here themselves, honey. I didn't know a thing about it. I've told them plenty of times before that I want it stopped, too. I'm going to do something far-fetched to them this time."

Corra turned and, without a word, walked straight to the door. She opened it, crossed the hall, and walked stiffly up the stairs.

Jeff followed her, his feet dragging with every step. His head moved from side to side as he led himself over the floor towards the door. He looked like a huge shaggy animal being drawn against his will. He mounted the steps behind his wife, wondering how long it was going to take him this time to convince her that he was as innocent of wrong-doing as a newborn pup.

CHAPTER VII

IT WAS the middle of the hot July morning, three
hours later, when Jeff finally left the bedroom on
the second floor of the jailhouse and came down the
stairs. He came down slowly, dropping one heavy foot
after another on the squeaky treads. It was a sound
like a sack of scrap iron falling each time the weight
of his body was lowered to another step.

There had been no shouting, there had been no
crashing of furniture upstairs during all the time. All
that had been heard down on the first floor was an in-
cessant humming, the kind of sound made by a single
person talking ceaselessly without inflection of the
voice. Bert had waited patiently in the office under
the bedroom until the monotonous drone lulled him
to sleep. He had even gone without his breakfast in
order to be on hand when Jeff came down.

Jeff reached the bottom step and moved heavily
across the hall towards the office door.

"Bert!" he yelled.

Bert jumped from the chair and ran to the door.

"Yes, sir, Sheriff Jeff," he said sleepily.

"Bert," he said wearily, stopping and looking at Bert in a strange way. "Bert, I'd give my soul if I had had the common ordinary sense to stay down on the farm when I was a young man. I'd heap rather be a frazzle-assed plowboy right this minute than be anything the political life will ever do for me."

"Yes, sir, Sheriff Jeff," Bert said, getting out of the way.

Jeff pushed his bulk through the narrow doorway. Bert hurried in behind him.

"There's somebody waiting to see you, Sheriff Jeff," he said.

Jeff looked across the room straight into the eyes of Mrs. Narcissa Calhoun. She had been standing by the window, but she was already coming towards him. Jeff tried to turn around, but she had reached him before he had a chance to make a lunge for the door. When he looked at her again, she had extended her arm and was pointing to a large bundle of papers on a chair.

"What do you want, Cissy?" he asked fearfully, his eyes bulging at the sight of the petition.

He made his way to his chair, clutching at the desk

for support until he could ease his weight down into a place of rest.

"I'm glad to hear you're doing the right thing, Sheriff McCurtain," she said, smiling at him with unmistakable meaning.

"What am I doing, Cissy?" he asked, perplexed.

"Letting the will of the people prevail, of course, Sheriff McCurtain. I'm proud of you."

He wondered how he could keep away from the dangerously thin ground that she was leading him to. Cissy came and sat down in the chair beside his desk.

"My wife read me that book you sold me, Cissy," he said, beaming at her hopefully. "She read it to me about a month ago, I reckon it was. Corra—" He paused and cocked his head to one side, listening to the faint sounds overhead. "It was the one about Christ coming back to earth and getting a job as automobile salesman, selling second-hand cars. Of course, it ain't none of my business if Christ wants to come down and do that. But if anybody was to ask me, I'd say there's too many of them broken-down rattle-traps tearing around the country as it is. If Christ wants to come down and sell machines, why can't he sell brand-new ones instead of them old junk-piles? I took the worst beating I ever had in my life once when I bought a second-hand car from a fellow. I didn't have it a week before the axle broke in half, but that was only the start. The radiator dropped off in the road one day while I was driving along. It was one thing right after another, just like that. Now, you take Sam Brinson, the colored man. Sam's easy bait for any old second-hand car, and everybody knows the trouble he gets into. Sam has worked himself down to skin-and-bones all his life just trying to keep four wheels spinning. And what has it all amounted to? Nothing. Sam's as—"

He sat up, looking around the room. He had forgotten about Sam Brinson.

"What's the matter?" Cissy asked, looking at him curiously.

"Nothing," he said. "Nothing much." He looked at Bert, but he realized Bert probably had not heard a word since Sam was taken away. "I was just thinking about that little book you sold me, Cissy."

He listened overhead, trying to detect any unusual sound Corra might make in the bedroom. He was not worried about her as long as the sounds of her movements were familiar. He dreaded the coming of the time when he would hear the sound of a trunk being shut decisively or of a suitcase being dropped heavily on the floor. When he left Corra upstairs, he was fairly positive he had let her talk herself into not leaving, but there was always the danger that she might argue herself into changing her mind.

He beckoned Bert to him and whispered in his ear.

"Go out and see if you can hear anything about Sam," he said, keeping his voice low enough to prevent Cissy from overhearing. "Come right back as soon as you can. I'm all upset about what they done to him."

Bert left the office.

"Well—" Cissy said impatiently.

"Look here, Cissy," Jeff said, turning and looking directly at her. "Who wrote that story about Christ coming back and selling second-hand cars? It wasn't you, was it?"

"No, I didn't write it, Sheriff McCurtain. I sell the book to people."

"Do other folks believe Christ came down here and sold those old cars like the story said?"

"I can't speak for the tracts," she said, moving uneasily in the chair, "but I stand up for the Bible."

Jeff glanced nervously at the ceiling.

"I didn't come here to talk about the tracts," Cissy said quickly.

"What did you come for?"

"The petition," she said, leaping to her feet and bringing the heavy bundle of papers to the desk and dropping it before him.

"Now, Cissy—" he began.

"These are dangerous times, Sheriff McCurtain," she said, leaning over the desk towards him. "You know what the world's like today. We've got to do something about it. We've got to send all the niggers back to Africa where they came from. They're multiplying so fast there won't be room for a white person to breathe in before long. The niggers—"

"Now, Cissy," he said helplessly, "a man like me holding political office can't afford—"

"I was raised up among colored people," she said, her eyes sparkling with an intense light, "and I've always treated them right. But that was before they started buying those awful Black Jesus Bibles with pictures in it making Christ look like a black nigger man—"

"That ain't no sin, Cissy," he protested. "It looks to me like the niggers has got just as much right to say Christ was a black as the brother whites has to say he was a white. There ain't no way of proving it either way, is there?"

122

The light in her eyes was more intense than ever.

"Well, he might have been a black, at that," Jeff said doggedly.

"Sheriff McCurtain, you'll never win another election in Julie County if you stand up for that," she said firmly. "If you don't sign this petition and help send every last nigger in the country back to Africa where they came from—"

"But they didn't all come from there, Cissy," he said hopefully. "There's been any number of niggers born right down the back alley from here. Two nigger babies was born down there only last month."

"I know," she said in exasperation, "but I'm talking about the nigger race. All of us whites is duty-bound to get together with Senator Ashley Dukes and send the nigger race back to Africa."

"Why?" he asked, unconvinced.

"Because!" Cissy said stubbornly.

They sat in silence, each staring at the other.

Jeff was wondering what had kept Bert so long, hoping that when he did get back he would have news that Sam Brinson had been turned loose unharmed. He knew Sam would be able to make his way back, but Jeff hoped Bert would know where he was so they could send a car for him. He hated to think of Sam's having to trudge fifteen or twenty miles through swamps and over rough ground.

He glanced up at the ceiling, cocking his head to one side and listening contentedly. Corra's footsteps were much lighter than they had been the last time he heard them. He leaned back in his chair with a feeling of relief.

Mrs. Narcissa Calhoun picked up the bulky petition and dropped it squarely before him. She turned back the cover and pointed to the typing on the first sheet.

"This is what you are duty-bound to sign, Sheriff McCurtain," she said, pointing to the page with her long finger.

"Now, Cissy—" he protested, looking at the words on the paper.

TO THE PRESIDENT OF THE U.S.A.:

WE, THE UNDERSIGNED UPSTANDING LAW-ABIDING CITIZENS AND QUALIFIED VOTERS OF JULIE COUNTY, GEORGIA, DO HEREBY RESPECTFULLY URGE AND ENTREAT YOU, THE RESPECTED PRESIDENT OF OUR COUNTRY, THE UNITED STATES OF AMERICA, TO SEND ALL MEMBERS OF THE COLORED RACE, INCLUDING MULATTOES, QUADROONS, OCTOROONS, AND ALL PERSONS HAVING ANY DEGREE OF NEGRO BLOOD, TO THE COUNTRY OF AFRICA WITHOUT UNDUE DELAY.

124

Jeff read it hurriedly the first time, going back afterward and looking painstakingly at each word until he realized what it meant.

"No, sir," he said emphatically, shaking his shaggy head from side to side, "I ain't in favor of doing a far-fetched thing like that. Maybe some colored people do have mean traits, but there are brother whites in this country a heap meaner than any nigger I ever saw. Now, you take Sam Brinson, the colored man. He's a no-account scoundrel, all the time trading and swapping worn-out old second-hand automobiles, but aside from that he's as companionable a fellow as you'll find in either race. I'd hate not to have him around. I'd feel lost if Sam wasn't here no more."

Narcissa backed away, regarding Jeff with deep-seated scorn.

"You ain't a nigger-lover, is you, Sheriff McCurtain?" she asked loudly, her eyes snapping and flashing.

Jeff got up as quickly as he could, shoving the petition across the desk. The bundle of papers fell on the floor.

Her face turned crimson with anger.

"There ain't no name you can think of to call me

that'll make me change my mind about the colored," he said staunchly.

Narcissa reached down and gathered up the papers hurriedly. With them in her arms she backed towards the door.

"I wouldn't put it past you to be the one who started all this rape-and-lynching talk," he told her. "How come it was you who was the know-it-all, anyhow? I'll bet a pretty you put that Barlow girl up to saying what she did!"

Narcissa reached the door.

"You just wait till election-time, Sheriff McCurtain!" she said threateningly. "The voters are going to turn on you like you was a black nigger yourself. You won't never be sheriff of Julie County again. I'm going straight and tell Judge Ben Allen about you. He'll fix it so you won't never hold another political office as long as you live. You just wait and see!"

Before he could reach her, she turned and ran out the hall and out into the yard. He followed her as far as the porch and watched her get into her car and drive off. Preacher Felts was in the front seat with her.

Jeff went back through the hall and opened the iron door that led into the cage-room.

"Bert!" he called, walking down the passageway and

looking into each cage as he went along. It was too much to hope that he would see Sam Brinson sitting in one of the cages, but he could not keep from looking. "Bert! Come here, Bert!"

When he got to the rear door, which was still open, he looked up the street. Bert was halfway between the jailhouse and the corner.

"Bert!" he shouted, walking out on the sidewalk. Bert ran towards him.

"I can't find out a thing about Sam, Sheriff Jeff," he said, discouraged. "There's plenty of people who know about it, but nobody knows what happened to him. I asked everybody I saw, too."

Jeff turned and walked through the jailhouse to his office. Bert followed dutifully.

"Most of the people I talked to seem to think we ought to give up hoping to see Sam alive again," Bert said. "They said the crowd with the hunt-fever wouldn't turn him loose unless they could find Sonny Clark, and they think Sonny got away."

The phone was ringing in the office when they got there. Bert took the receiver off the hook, holding it indecisively while he waited for Jeff to tell him what to do about it.

"Go ahead and answer it," Jeff said wearily. "It's

likely another of them cockalorums ordering me to come out to Flowery Branch and make people stop scaring their biddies."

"Hello," Bert said into the phone. "Sheriff McCurtain's office."

He turned abruptly, his face blanched.

"It's Judge Ben Allen!"

"Oh, Lord!" Jeff breathed, closing his eyes for a few moments of restful peace.

Bert laid the phone on the desk and backed quietly away. Jeff moved himself across the floor to the desk.

"Hello, Judge," he said, forcing himself to speak up brightly.

"McCurtain, why didn't you get out to Flowery Branch last night after you left my house?"

"Judge, a lot of things happened last night, all of them pure wrong. If I had more time, I could explain them. It looked like all the power in the world was against me. I ain't been so plagued by so many far-fetched things all at the same time since God-come-Wednesday."

There was a long pause over the wires.

"*Consuetudo manerii et loci est observanda*," Judge Ben Allen said wearily.

"What's that, Judge?" Jeff asked quickly.

There was an even longer pause before Judge Allen spoke again.

"After getting a few scattered reports from around the county, the situation looks different than it did last night. It's too early yet to make a forecast, but maybe it'll be best if you lie low for a few hours. By that time I'll have a better line on the situation. It's a good thing you didn't get out to Flowery Branch, but I still don't understand why you didn't make straight for the country like I told you."

"It ain't so easy to try to explain over the phone, Judge. But I'm glad I wasn't needed out there, after all. I want to do my best to keep this lynching politically clean, Judge. If Mrs. Narcissa Calhoun would only keep out—"

"You stay where you are, McCurtain, so I can put my hands on you when I want you. I don't want to hear of you going off fishing, or nothing like that. Good-by."

"Good-by, Judge," Jeff said weakly, replacing the receiver on the hook.

He turned and looked at Bert standing between him and the window. Bert's face was pale and solemn.

"Bert," he said, "sometimes I don't know if I'm coming or going. If you'll take my advice, you'll get out of politics and never let yourself be tempted to sample a pollbook as long as you live. If I was you, I'd marry myself a loving wife and settle down to a peaceful way of living out on a little farm somewhere."

"Why, Sheriff Jeff?"

"Because, Bert. Because!"

He got up painfully, pushing the sides of the chair from his hips. Once on his feet, he looked up at the ceiling, listening intently for Corra's sounds. All was as quiet and peaceful as summer twilight. There was a faint aroma of boiling vegetables in the air. He tilted back his head, his nostrils flaring, and breathed deeply of it. He moved towards the door.

"I'm worried sick about Sam Brinson, the colored man," he said. "As soon as I get a little bite to eat, I'm going to do some inquiring about him. I just can't sit still and let something far-fetched happen to Sam."

Bert got out of his way. He moved through the door and went to the bottom of the stairway in the hall. He listened for a moment before beginning to climb the stairs. Just as he mounted the first step, Corra came out of the bedroom and went into the kitchen. Jeff went on up, his nostrils quivering at the odor of boiling beans and freshly baked cornbread.

CHAPTER VIII

SHEP BARLOW, his eyes bloodshot from loss of sleep, got back home at noon that day. He had been away, alone, since the evening before. His blue-black beard, which was already three days old when he left, was a mat of bristly stubble. Shep was a wiry little five-foot man, and his insignificant-looking stature made his face seem awesome in contrast.

The six or eight men standing under the umbrella tree in the front yard spoke to him cautiously as he went past. Everyone else had left, most of them to search for the Negro, some to eat dinner. The crowd had become restless and angry at the delay caused by Shep's failure to come back within a reasonable length of time. He had told them not to do anything until he came back, and the men had expected him to be there by sunrise. A large party had gone to Oconee Swamp, while a smaller group had gone in the opposite direction towards Earnshaw Ridge. Those who remained at the house were disgusted with the dilatory methods still being used eighteen hours after the word had spread over the county.

Shep had hoped to find Sonny single-handed. He wanted to be the one to catch him, because he wished to have the satisfaction of tying a rope around the Negro boy's neck and dragging him behind his car through the country before turning him over to the crowd. But during all that time he had not found a trace of Sonny.

The men under the tree watched Shep cross the yard. One or two of them spoke to him, but he did not even turn his head in reply. They knew by his behavior that he had not found Sonny, and that he was dangerously out of sorts.

After stomping up the front steps and across the porch, Shep threw his hat on the floor in the hall and walked into the dining-room.

He stopped abruptly at the door. A strange man sat at the table eating dinner with Katy. Shep was surprised to find a stranger there, although the longer he stared, the more certain he became that he had seen the man before. The stranger had a long white beard that reached almost to the top button on his trousers.

His shirt-front was completely covered by the bushy hair.

The old man raised a spoonful of blackeyed peas in his shaking hand, but before putting it into his mouth he parted the beard carefully around his lips.

"Who's that?" Shep demanded, coming slowly into the room and taking a long close look at him. "Who's he, Katy?"

"It's Grandpa Harris, Papa," she said. "You haven't forgotten him, have you?"

"I thought I told him to stay away from here," he said to no one in particular.

Shep went to his chair at the head of the table, his eyes blazing.

"Where'd he come from?" he asked. He stood behind his chair for several moments before sitting down. "What does he want?"

The old man put down his spoon and looked up at Shep over the rim of his glasses. His beard grew in a peculiar sort of way, making him look as if he were grinning about something all the time. The snowy white hair on each side of his face grew in whorls under his cheek bones and then flowed down to his waist in folds like crinkled white tissue-paper.

"Howdy, son," he said to Shep, speaking for the first time.

To look at him, there was no way of knowing whether he was actually smiling, or whether it was the beard that made him look as if he were. It made Shep angry to be grinned at like that.

Shep jerked out his chair and sat down without answering him. He filled his plate with blackeyed peas and began shoveling them into his mouth. It did not make him feel any better when he reached across the table with his fork to spear a piece of cornbread and found that it had all been eaten.

Grandpa Harris, with what looked to Shep like unseemly glee under the circumstances, parted his beard and took another mouthful of peas.

"Grandpa Harris walked all the way over here from Smith County when he heard what happened last night," Katy spoke up.

"Heard what happened?"

"Why, Papa, the raping, of course."

"I don't believe there was no raping done around here, last night or no other time," he said surlily. "That woman who sells the tracts and you made up that tale. I ain't found no trace of that nigger you said done it. It's all a big lie."

Katy caught her breath, looking at the two men bewilderedly. She did not know what to say.

"I ain't seen Katy since the time her mother died," Grandpa Harris said. "When the word reached me, I started out for here right away. I wanted to see Katy one more time before I went."

"Went where?" Shep asked, looking at him.

"Went to die," Grandpa Harris said. "I'm getting old."

Shep studied him casually, his mouth curling.

"You're pretty old to be traveling around the country like this," he said. "Old people like you ought to stay at home where you belong." He became angrier as he spoke. "I told you once before I didn't want to see you around here again."

"I don't aim to be a burden on you, son," the man said. "I'll be starting back to Smith County before long. I just wanted to see Annie's girl a little. I don't reckon I'll ever have another chance to see her."

"See to it that you don't forget to go back then," Shep said, turning to his meal and lowering his head over his plate of blackeyed peas.

Grandpa Harris looked at Shep and Katy, but there was still no way of knowing whether he was angry or grinning under the beard. The whorls of white hair on his cheeks appeared to be spinning around like a pinwheel in a breeze. The last time he was there, the time he was ordered to stay away, he had walked all the way from Smith County to attend his daughter's funeral. That was when he had threatened to send for the sheriff if Shep did not take Annie's body from the well and give her a decent burial. Shep had chased him off the place within five minutes after the funeral was over and had ordered him never to set foot in the house again.

"I don't aim to put nobody to trouble over me," Grandpa Harris said, grinning and chewing. He parted his beard as he took three spoonfuls of peas in quick succession. "Just as soon as I see Katy for a little while, I'll quit and start back home. I don't reckon I've got a right to say it, son, but just the same I hope nothing shameful happens over this trouble of Katy's."

Shep sat up, knocking his spoon from his plate.

"What in hell do you mean by that?" he demanded.

"Son, it would be a lot better to let the sheriff of the county take charge of this trouble, because I don't like for Annie's girl to be mixed up in a shameful lynching. I know if Annie was here, she'd say the same thing."

"You keep your mouth out of this," Shep said. "Nobody is going to come butting into my business and tell me that a nigger can rape my womenfolks and get away with it."

Shep shoved his plate away and got up noisily.

"Now, son—" Grandpa Harris said calmly.

Halfway to the door Shep turned and shouted at Katy.

"Where's that Calhoun woman?"

"She went away right after breakfast, Papa. She said she had some work to do somewhere else."

He turned and glared at Grandpa Harris. The old man was cleaning and stroking his silky white beard with his handkerchief.

"You keep out of my business," he shouted at him. "I don't want to hear no more talk about turning this thing over to the sheriff. If Jeff McCurtain comes sticking his nose into my business, I'll make him wish he'd never seen a ballot-box. I'd shoot McCurtain down as quick as I'd shoot that nigger I'm looking for."

He turned from Grandpa Harris and glared threateningly at his daughter.

"I don't want to find you siding with him, do you hear me! I'm your paw, and you do what I tell you!"

Katy nodded quickly, drawing away from him.

Before she could get out of the way, her father had grabbed her with his left hand and had struck her with his right. His fist struck her on the side of her head, sending her crashing against the wall.

He looked down at her sprawled at his feet for a moment and then turned and walked out of the house.

Two automobiles filled with men had driven into the yard a few minutes before. Another car could be seen a quarter of a mile away, jolting over the rough road.

Shep stood in the yard looking across the fields choked with grass. His cotton was stunted and starved. In another few days his crop would be too far gone to save. Almost everyone else in that section of the country had finished laying-by, and he wondered what Bob Watson would say and do if he should happen to see one of his tenant's crops in that condition.

Several men came across the yard while he was looking at the grass in the field.

"Howdy, Shep," one of the men said.

"Howdy," he answered without looking at them.

There was silence for a while. The noonday sun beat down unrelentingly. All the men looked at the grass-choked cotton without comment.

The car that had been coming up the lane towards

the house reached the yard. Several men got out carrying shotguns and rifles.

One of the men standing around Shep nudged him with an elbow.

"We've been thinking, Shep," he said haltingly. "And we want to ask you a question."

Shep turned on his heel.

"What!" he said angrily.

"You didn't say anything to the sheriff about this, did you, Shep?"

"Hell, no!" he shouted, glaring at the faces around him.

The tension on the men's faces vanished.

"What we waiting for, then?" one of them said, throwing his shotgun under his arm. "If a nigger raped one of my womenfolks, I'd shoot every last one of them in the whole country till I got the right one."

"The sheriff will be out here with bloodhounds, taking that nigger right out from under our noses, if we don't stir around and grab him first," another man said.

"No sheriff is going to take that nigger while I'm alive," Shep said.

"That's the way to talk, Shep!"

Shep pushed the men out of his way and went towards the road where the cars were standing.

"There's a big crowd down in Oconee Swamp," one of the men said, running and catching up with him. "And there's quite a sizable crowd over in them woods on the side of Earnshaw Ridge. What you figure on doing, Shep? That nigger can't be in but one place at a time. Where do you figure he's at?"

Shep did not reply.

"A lot of them got tired waiting for you to come back this morning, and they split up into bunches to go out looking. I stuck right here waiting for you, Shep, because I don't believe in quarreling at a time like this."

Katy came out on the porch, looking at the men scattered over the yard. She went to the post beside the steps and leaned against it. Two or three of the men turned around and watched her. She smiled at them.

A man who had been sitting alone in one of the cars got out and crossed the yard to meet Shep. It was Clint Huff, a carpenter, from Andrewjones.

"Hold on, Clint," somebody said. "You and Shep ain't got no cause to scrap each other at a time like this. A white girl's been—"

Clint pushed him aside and went towards Shep. He and Shep had been quarreling and fighting since they were old enough to carry knives. The last time they had come together was at the sheriff's annual barbecue the summer before. Shep had a scar three inches long on his chest to remind him of it.

They faced each other, keeping a distance between them.

"What you mean by trying to get this lynching party all balled up?" Clint said. "You act like you're trying to boss it, don't you?"

Clint drew his knife from his pocket and opened the blade.

"Now, wait a minute, Clint," somebody said, stepping between them. "This ain't no way to catch a nigger. Besides, everybody's got a clear chance at catching him, anyway."

Clint shoved the man out of the way. Shep still had not said anything, but he had put his hand into his pocket and was drawing his knife.

"You must be hiding that nigger out somewhere for Jeff McCurtain," Clint said. He turned and glanced swiftly at the men around him. "Any man who'll turn a raping nigger over to the sheriff ain't no better than a nigger himself."

Shep snapped open the blade of his knife with a quick jerk of his fingers.

The men tried to draw Clint and Shep apart, but both of them fought off all efforts to keep them separated. They were facing each other at less than five paces.

Shep crouched a little, gripping his knife in his fist. Clint threw his hat on the ground and advanced on Shep in a circular direction.

All the men in the yard crowded as close as they could, knowing by then that it was useless to try to stop them until they had fought awhile. Everyone was so preoccupied in watching the two men that nobody noticed Grandpa Harris when he pushed through the ring of men and ran into the center of the circle. It was too late then to do anything, because the moment he got there, both Clint and Shep lunged forward. The impact knocked Grandpa Harris from his feet and sent him crashing to the ground.

First Clint, and then Shep, backed away. They did not know what had happened, but Grandpa Harris had not moved since he struck the ground. The men crowded around Shep and Clint, drawing them apart. When they were on the opposite side of the yard from each other, some of the others lifted Grandpa Harris and carried him to the porch. He was stretched out on his back.

"What happened to Grandpa Harris?" Katy said excitedly, getting down beside him.

"He ran right into the middle of it," somebody said. "I reckon he was trying to stop it. He ain't bleeding that I can see. He'll come to in a little while and be all right. Anyway, old men like him ain't got no business rushing into places like that. If one of them knives had struck him, he wouldn't be here now."

Both Clint and Shep were shouting, but they were being kept far enough apart to prevent either one of them from jumping on the other. The men were talking to them, trying to persuade them to give up their knives for the rest of the day.

"Grandpa Harris ran right past me," Katy said excitedly, "but I didn't know what he was going to do. I could've stopped him, I reckon."

Somebody drew her away while the old man was being lifted from the porch. They carried him inside and laid him on a bed. Katy stayed with him for a few minutes, but she wanted to see the men in the yard, and she came back to the porch.

Clint shook off the men who were trying to hold

him and went to his car. He got into it and drove off alone.

The crowd moved across the yard, following Shep to the porch. He sat down on the steps, muttering to himself.

"That was a shame about the old man, Shep," somebody said. "But I reckon he'll come to after a while. Looks like he would've had better sense than to go busting right into the middle of a fight like that, though."

Shep did not answer.

"Who is that old codger, anyway?"

Shep shook his head.

"It was an accident, anyway. It would've happened to anybody who happened to get in the middle of you and Clint Huff."

Shep got up, looked around for a moment, and went straight to the corner of the porch where he had left his shotgun when he came home.

He did not say anything as he hurried to his car. The men knew that the hunt was on.

CHAPTER IX

KATY BARLOW, flushed and breathless, was so mad she could spit.

Tossing her hair out of her eyes and brushing it back from her face, she drew her lips tightly against her teeth. She wished she could turn into a man so she could do it all the better.

She thought of all the different ways she could spit if she were a man. She would spit between her feet, and over her shoulder, and straight into the air. She would even spit at Leroy Luggit's face.

Leroy, up there squat on the seat in the cab of the logging truck like a devil on a throne, grinned down at her mockingly. While she glared at him fiercely, stamping first one foot and then the other, Leroy raised his hand slowly and pushed the goggles up on his forehead.

White circles around his eyes looked at her as mockingly as the scoffing grin on his face. He wore goggles to keep the dust out of his eyes while he was hauling logs from Earnshaw Ridge to the sawmill down in the Oconee lowland. With his goggles pushed up on his forehead, Leroy looked as if he were jeering her with four eyes instead of only two.

"I'm spitting mad, Leroy Luggit!" she cried at him, stamping her feet in the road.

He laughed at her, throwing back his head and slapping the steeringwheel with both hands.

"I've never been so spitting-mad before in all my life, Leroy Luggit!"

She could see no resemblance in him then to the man who had met her at Flowery Branch bridge only a short week before and had given her a large bag of orange-flavored gumdrops that he bought especially for her in Andrewjones.

Katy thrust one foot forward, placing it carefully on the step of the truck; then she leaned as close to Leroy as she could reach, and spat with all her might at his face.

Minute after minute went by while they stared each other in the eyes, but it seemed to Katy as if everything in the world had stopped. She was as surprised at herself as was Leroy at what had happened. She had never spat in a person's face before in all her life.

She had never even dreamed of doing a thing like that. It made her tremble to realize what she had done.

Slowly he began to wipe his face with his shirt-sleeves, one arm passing over his face after another, while the skin up to the roots of his hair became scarlet and swollen with a rising surge of blood.

Katy made as if to spit at him again. Then she heard him shout at her as he jumped from the truck.

"You hell-cat you! You black-haired hell-cat, you!"

She moved backward towards the side of the road, spitting at him with each step she took.

"I told you I was mad, Leroy Luggit!" she screamed angrily. "Nobody's got a right to talk to me like you did a little while ago! I won't stand for it! Do you hear me, Leroy Luggit!"

She kept moving slowly backward, still spitting with almost every step she took.

Leroy glared at her with flaming anger. His scarlet-colored face was wet with perspiration which seemed to ooze from every pore in his skin.

"You may think you're mad," he said between gritted teeth, "but it's not nothing to what I am!"

"If you do anything to me, Leroy Luggit," she said threateningly, "I'll tell Papa on you." She retreated guardedly. "I'll tell him what you did to me at the bridge, too. You just wait and see if I don't!"

"I ain't scared of him or nobody else," he said, sneering.

He continued to advance upon her step by step.

"I'll tell everybody in the world on you!" she cried desperately. "I'll tell Sheriff McCurtain and Judge Ben Allen and Mrs. Narcissa Calhoun!"

"No female is going to spit in my face and get away with it!" he shouted at her.

With a swiftness she did not know she was capable of, she reached down and scooped up a handful of dust. The dust was yellow and powdery, and she had trouble keeping it from flowing between her fingers. She gripped it with all her might.

Leroy swung his arms at his side threateningly. Katy's grip on the dust tightened.

"You ain't been raped," he said, looking her straight in the eyes. "Hell, no! You're bragging! Or else you turned on that nigger boy because he wouldn't lay out with you. You ain't been raped, Katy Barlow."

She spat at his face as hard as she could.

"You shut your mouth, Leroy Luggit!" she cried at him.

"They ought to do something to you for lying about

it. Females like you ought to be beaten till you can't see straight. I've got a good mind—"

He drew an arm across his face, wiping away the perspiration with his shirtsleeve.

"You're nothing to be scared of, Leroy Luggit," she said, trembling as she tried to hide her fright. "You can't scare me with that kind of talk."

"You'd better be scared," he said, going towards her, "because I'm going to beat the life out of you."

She waited alertly where she was, her eyes fixed on Leroy's hands. He came closer, and when he was only four or five feet from her, and when she dared not to wait any longer, she threw the handful of dust into his eyes and, turning, ran like a young fox through the patch of Jimson weeds beside the road.

As she ran she could hear him cursing her, but she did not dare look back over her shoulder until she felt she was a safe distance away. When she saw him standing in the road, she stopped and turned around. He stood where he had stopped in his tracks when the dust blinded him, digging at his eyes and cursing her at the top of his voice.

Katy shuddered as she looked at him. She knew he was angry enough to hurt her if he could have got his hands on her, and he was strong enough to do anything once he had her in his grasp. She was glad she had thought of scooping up a handful of dust and throwing it into his eyes. He might even have killed her right there in the road before he had finished. While she was thinking about it, she began walking slowly backward until there was an even greater distance between them.

While she watched him try to rub the dust from his eyes, the things he had said to her earlier, the things that had made her so angry, began coming back to her and reminding her of his scornful attitude. The words he had spoken rang in her ears maddeningly.

"Why don't you stop being a slut and get yourself a man who'll keep you, Katy?" he had said. She even remembered how he had looked when he said it. His face was solemn and earnest, but he had the manner of scorn about him. "I can't afford to take chances with you any longer. I'd be a fool to drink water out of every tin can I found lying beside the road, anyway. That's what I mean. You're nothing but a cotton-field slut."

The blood rose in her face as the words came back to her.

"You ought to be ashamed of yourself for letting people lynch a little nigger boy that's as innocent as the day is long. If I thought you was telling the truth about it, I'd be out there with the rest of them tracking him down. Lynching would be too good for him, if there was any truth in it. But you don't see me out there doing it, do you?"

She had believed for a long time that she and Leroy were going to be married. Only a few weeks before that they had talked about renting a vacant house on Earnshaw Ridge and buying some bedroom and dining-room furniture on weekly payments at the store in Andrewjones. They were afraid that her father would not give his consent, because she was so young, but they had several plans for running away to be married. At that very minute at home there was a dress she had been making secretly, keeping it hidden from her father in a cardboard box under her bed. The dress was only half finished, but in the bottom of the box there were six napkins she had cut and hemmed and two towels that she had embroidered. Wrapped up in a piece of cloth in one corner of the box was the money she had saved with which to buy muslin for their wedding sheet the next time she went to the store. Tears filled her eyes. She brushed them away in order to be able to watch Leroy.

She had waited for nearly two hours for him to

come along the road. It was almost sundown when she finally heard the noise of his logging truck as it rumbled over the wooden bridge at Flowery Branch. Then she jumped up and stood in the middle of the road waving to him. She thought at the time that he looked glad to see her. She had almost cried with joy when he smiled at her.

"Hello, Katy," he had said.

"Aren't you going to get out, Leroy?" she had asked impatiently, wanting his arms around her.

He was silent then. It frightened her.

"Leroy!"

She smiled at him bravely, trying to hide the fear that had come over her.

That was when he had shaken his head, leaning back in his seat. He had scorned her.

She looked down the road at him now, digging at the stinging yellow dust in his eyes. He had torn off his goggles and thrown them away. He seemed to think she was somewhere near, because he was still shouting curses at her.

"You're nothing but a cotton-field slut," he had said.

That was what had hurt her almost as much as being scorned. Her face felt hot and dry when she remembered it.

The sun was going down, looking as though it had suddenly grown tired after the long day. Towards the east the country was beginning to look cool and peaceful. There was a small dark cloud drifting towards the sun on the horizon. In a few moments the cloud began turning crimson and gold as the sun's rays struck it. For an instant the whole western sky looked as if the world were on fire; then the sun sank out of sight, leaving the cloud dark and lifeless. The air moved a little, for the first time that day, and the branches on the trees swayed, rustling the heavy green leaves.

Katy had forgotten about Leroy momentarily. She turned quickly and saw him down the road fifty yards away. He had straightened up, and he was no longer cursing her. He watched her walk through the knee-high weeds and circle through the field towards the road.

She knew he was through with her. She could tell by the way she felt, by the way he had looked at her, by the way he had spoken to her, and by the way the air she breathed seared her parched throat. She was sorry she had allowed herself to hide beside the road and catch Sonny Clark when he walked past, that she had permitted Mrs. Narcissa Calhoun to spread a story of rape over the country, that she had stood on the front porch and exposed herself to the crowd of men in the front yard. Leroy knew the truth about all of it. That was why he had scorned her. He was through with her.

He was looking up the road at her then. She began walking backward away from him. Leroy slapped some of the dust out of his trousers and opened the door of his truck. He was still looking at her when he climbed inside.

After Leroy had gone, she began to feel alone. Before she knew it, she had begun to cry. Fighting her way to the side of the road, with cool streams of tears flowing over her burning skin, she reached out and grasped her arms full of weeds and bushes. She had to have something to hold onto. Then she sank to the ground, putting her face down against her knees, and wrapping her arms around her head. She had never felt so lonely before. She sobbed, wishing her mother were alive so she could go to her. She felt if she could lose herself in her mother's arms she would be able to endure the pain that was so intense she could not keep from screaming. For a long time she cried brokenly, hugging herself with her arms, and tried to keep from thinking of the things she had made and kept in the scarlet-colored cardboard box under her bed.

She tried to stop thinking about all the things that filled her mind. After that the only thing she could feel was that she did not want to live any longer. She wished she were dead. She was sorry she had not stayed in the road when Leroy threatened her. If she had stayed, she would not have to lie where she was and endure such pain.

Twilight had vanished when she opened her eyes and raised her head. Sudden fear in her mind made her jump to her feet. She looked all around at the close darkness. She was not sure whether she had fallen asleep in a dream, but whatever it was, she thought somebody was creeping towards her in the night. Screaming, she ran up the road, not daring to look behind her.

When she had exhausted herself, she stopped, panting painfully. Her heart beat against her chest until it was almost unbearable. She looked down the road behind without being able to see whether anyone was following her or not. She could hear no sounds anywhere, but she felt as if somebody in the darkness were watching her. She turned and ran up the road as fast as she could, screaming. She fell almost as fast as she could get back on her feet.

No matter how fast she was able to run, she could not get away from the fear that gripped her. She felt as if somebody in the darkness somewhere around her would at any moment strike her down with savage force. She lost the road in the darkness, finding herself stumbling and falling headlong into a thicket of briars. She struggled to her feet and ran on, torn and bleeding, in a final effort to escape.

CHAPTER X

AFTER a good long undisturbed afternoon nap, Jeff
McCurtain went downstairs to the office to find
out if anything out of the ordinary had happened
between noon and dark. It was the first time in several
weeks that he had been able to take a long uninter-
rupted nap during the day. It usually happened that
when he felt like dozing in the afternoon, he was con-
tinually being waked up to serve an attachment or a
writ on some farmer living in the farthest corner of
the county.

Bert was waiting for him at the foot of the stairway.
He followed Jeff into the office.

"Anything happen?" he asked Bert.

"Nothing at all, Sheriff Jeff," Bert said. "It's been
quiet all afternoon. You didn't have to get up from
your nap unless you wanted to. Me and Jim are watching over things."

Jeff looked around the office and promptly walked

out again. He went to the porch, feeling rested and calm.

The street lights had just been turned on, and the flickering rays filled him with a desire to go back to bed. Corra would be getting into bed before long, and he could lie there with her beside him and forget the worries of the outside world. The following day was Saturday, and there was certain to be a whole new batch of court papers to serve.

Bert appeared beside him.

"They haven't found him yet, Sheriff Jeff," Bert said, startling him.

"Haven't found who yet?"

"That nigger boy," Bert said, surprised.

"Oh," Jeff said, looking out into the street.

After a few moments he turned to Bert.

"But Sam's back, ain't he?"

"No, Sheriff Jeff. It looks like Sam Brinson has disappeared completely. Nobody in town has heard a thing about him."

"That's bad," Jeff said slowly. "That's real bad."

He walked to the corner of the porch and looked up at the sky. The stars were out bright and thick. It was too early for the moon.

"How about Judge Ben Allen?" he asked. "Has he phoned?"

"No, sir," Bert said.

Jeff was silent, thinking.

"That nigger boy's been at large long enough to be caught long before this," he said after a while. "I sure would like to know what's holding things up this way."

"He's only been at large for twenty-four hours, Sheriff Jeff," Bert reminded him. "The trouble only started about this time last night. They'll probably catch him by morning."

"I reckon you must be right about the time, but I feel like I've already been through a week of worry. But Sam Brinson, the colored man, has been gone far too long. I'm worried about Sam."

Bert did not say anything. He waited to hear if Jeff had any instructions for him.

"I sure would give a lot to know what happened to Sam," Jeff said, gazing at the lights flickering on the pavement. "Now, people just ain't got no right to carry off a human being like that. It's a penal offense to abduct a law-abiding citizen, even darkies. Sam hadn't harmed a soul in the world. He's gentle-minded. He never went out to do a person harm."

Jeff walked up and down the porch several times,

his forehead wrinkled in thought. Bert hovered by the door in case Jeff called him. It was another five minutes before Jeff stopped his pacing up and down.

"Get me my hat, Bert," he said quickly, going down the steps towards his car parked in the street. "I want you to drive me out to Flowery Branch. I'm going to make some inquiries around."

"But, Sheriff Jeff—"

"Get me my hat like I said!"

When Bert came out of the jailhouse with the hat, Jeff was sitting in the car waiting. Bert got under the steeringwheel.

"Bert, me and you is going off on an unofficial trip to attend to some unfinished business. It ain't political. It's pure personal business."

He pointed his hand in the direction of the road to Flowery Branch, motioning to Bert to start the car.

They drove slowly out of town and a few minutes later they were in the country rolling along behind a beam of sharp white light that pushed the darkness back on each side of the road. There were few lighted windows along the way, even though it was early in the evening. Several times they passed dwellings that revealed only a thin crack of light under the doors. All the Negro cabins were closed and dark. They looked as if they had been boarded up and deserted.

They met several cars along the road during the next half-hour, all of them moving slowly. Once they came upon a group of men around a bend in the road. The twelve or fifteen persons dashed for the bushes beside the road when the headlights suddenly flashed upon them. They had been standing around a smudge fire. The smoke had drifted ahead for several hundred yards, and Jeff and Bert drove through wisps of it during the next few minutes.

As they approached Flowery Branch bridge, a dull glow of light appeared. After going a little closer, they could see a jumbled mass of cars that looked as if they had been hastily stopped and left where they happened to be. Many of the cars were standing with their headlights burning. There were several almost upon the bridge.

"Hold on, Bert," Jeff said anxiously. He sat up and peered ahead uneasily. "Switch off the lights and drive slow."

They crept along the road until they were only a few yards from the nearest automobiles. There were no men within sight, but up at the bridge many voices could be heard.

"Reckon they got him, Sheriff Jeff?" Bert asked

nervously, trying to keep his voice in a low whisper.

"Got who?" Jeff asked.

"Sonny."

"I don't know," he said impatiently.

He motioned to Bert to drive off to one side. As soon as the car came to a stop, Jeff opened the door and got out.

"I ain't forgetting myself," he said defensively. "I still aim to keep this lynching politically clean. But I'm worried about Sam."

Instead of walking up the road, they tramped in a roundabout way through the brush to a point that was within sight of the bridge. Standing where they were, they were fairly safe from detection. Several of the men were talking loudly. Bert and Jeff stood behind a hickory tree and tried to overhear what was being said.

Even at that distance they could recognize by sight several men they knew. Shep Barlow and Clint Huff were in the center of the bridge facing each other. The rest of the men were crowded behind them.

"I'm running this shooting-match," Shep was heard to say. "If nobody don't like the way I'm running it, then get to hell away from here. I'm running it as I God damn please."

Clint Huff moved several steps.

"What you mean by stopping that car of yours in the middle of the road and blocking everything?" he said angrily. "This ain't no way to catch a nigger. My old woman could do better at it than you're doing. All this shouting and yelling gives him the best chance in the world to get away from here. Get that car of yours out of the way!"

Clint moved closer to Shep.

"Get that God damn car of yours out of the road, Barlow!" he shouted. "I ain't going to stand here all night waiting for you to sober up. I'll knock you off this bridge, if you don't move to do something about it."

Jeff nudged Bert.

"They're arguing over the Clark nigger," Jeff said in a whisper. "It ain't the same bunch that took Sam off."

Shep had backed up against the bridge railing.

"I'm running this shooting-match just like I said," he shouted, waving his arms in the air. "Everybody who wants to catch the nigger, fall in with me!"

Nobody moved.

"I ain't taking no orders from no drunk," Clint said.

163

"If that car of yours ain't moved out of the way, I'm going to ram it out with a truck."

The two men faced each other while the crowd moved closer in order to get a better view.

"This is the damnedest nigger-hunt I ever saw," one of the men in the crowd said. "Everybody squabbling, and the nigger hotfooting it away from here as fast as his legs will carry him. This ain't no way to catch him at all."

"Let Shep Barlow alone! He knows what he's doing!"

"I'm putting my money on Clint!"

"This is a hell of a way to catch a nigger!"

"This ain't no nigger-hunt—this here's a jawing-match!"

Clint reached into his pocket for his knife, but before he could draw it, Shep lunged forward, butting him down. Clint fell sprawling on his back.

"Don't let him pull that knife on you, Shep!" somebody shouted warningly. "He'll rip you open like a hog!"

"Shut up and let them fight it out. Shep Barlow can take care of himself, drunk or sober. I've seen him fight before when he was drunk."

The barber from Andrewjones rushed at Shep with

a monkey wrench. Before he could strike Shep, somebody had shoved him towards the railing. He went tumbling over out of sight.

"God damn it, this ain't no way for you folks to be doing!" somebody said. "You folks save up and do your scrapping tomorrow or some other time. I came out here to help track down a nigger."

Somebody picked Clint up and pushed him towards one of the cars. Fifteen or twenty men followed behind.

"What we going to do now, Shep?" several of them asked.

Shep brushed himself off and started for his car. The men on the bridge began arguing among themselves, some of them undecided whether to follow Clint or Shep.

Jeff and Bert backed away and circled around through the brush until they were back where the car had been left. Jeff was hurrying across the ditch when a flashlight was turned on him. Several men crowded around him.

"What the hell are you doing out here, McCurtain?" one of them demanded. "I think it's pretty funny to be stumbling over you out here where you don't have no business of being. You ain't fixing to double-cross nobody, is you?"

Two of the men began roughing Bert, pushing him towards the road.

"Why ain't you laying low like Judge Ben Allen told you to do?" one of the others asked. "I talked to Judge Ben Allen on the phone, and he told me—"

"Now, hold on a minute," Jeff said uneasily. "There ain't no use in anybody in the whole wide world misunderstanding me. I've worked myself frazzle-assed trying to keep this lynching politically clean. That's why I wouldn't be out here on false pretenses. All I wanted to do was find what became of Sam—"

"Sam who?"

"Sam Brinson, the colored man," Jeff said. "Everybody knows Sam. He's the darky who's always trading old machines and getting into hot water every now and then about the mortgages. Some folks carried Sam off, and I started out to hear some word of him."

"That ain't no reason to find you snooping around out here when we're looking for that Clark nigger, McCurtain."

"Now, boys," Jeff pleaded, "don't jump so hard-almighty at conclusions. I thought somebody around here might know about him. He was carried away from the jailhouse early this morning, but he ain't got a thing in the world to do with this trouble. He gets into a fix now and then when he sells one of them old cars of his when it ain't clear of mortgage, but he don't mean no harm."

"This is a bad season of the year for any nigger to be getting into trouble," a man said. "It ain't healthy for that Brinson nigger, or any of them, to be crossing white people right now."

"Sam never sets out to do harm," Jeff protested. "It just looks like it's pure second-nature with him to be wanting to swap them old machines of his around."

"Well, he ain't out here, McCurtain," a gruff voice broke in. "And the best place for you at a time like this is right back at the jailhouse in Andrewjones."

Jeff moved towards his car by the side of the road. The men walked on each side of him in silence. Jeff did not like the careless manner of some of them with their shotguns and rifles, and he watched them nervously.

Several other men came up suddenly out of the darkness, but no one said anything. The faces in the light looked grim and determined.

Bert was standing in the ditch with half a dozen

men around him holding guns in the crooks of their arms. He looked worried.

"All right, McCurtain," somebody prompted him. "Remember the talk we had back there a minute ago."

He and Bert got into the car. The men, fifteen or twenty of them by that time, waited in a semicircle while Bert started the engine and drove down the road in the direction of Andrewjones.

Bert ventured to speak after they had gone two or three miles. He had waited as long as he could before saying anything.

"Maybe we ought to be going back to the jailhouse toreckly," he suggested. "There's no telling where Jim Couch is, and somebody ought to be there in case something comes up."

Jeff motioned to him to slow down the car. Bert stopped it at once on the side of the road.

"Hot blast it," Jeff said with sudden determination, "I ain't going to let a crowd of lawbreaking citizens stop me from locating Sam. No! We ain't going back to town now, or toreckly, either. I'd never get over it if something far-fetched happened to Sam Brinson. Let's just sit here in the cool of the night for a little while till I can think it over properly. I've

already made up my mind I ain't going to budge myself back to town till I find out what in the world
became of that darky. I'm going to stick at it if it takes
till God-come-Wednesday."

CHAPTER XI

THE MOON came up full and bright from the dark
depths of the piney woods. Powdery yellow dust,
blown into the air by many automobiles speeding over
the unpaved roads, was settling in layers over the flat
land. The dark green leaves on the bushes beside the
road were stained with the yellow dust, but in the
bright moonlight they sparkled lazily with dew as the
hot summer air drifted without direction from one
field to the next. The country was quiet and hushed,
with only the occasional barking of a dog afar off in
the distance to be heard.

Bert had waited silently on the seat beside Jeff, waiting for him to speak again, for almost half an hour.
He took out his watch and glanced at it.

"I don't like to speak about it again, Sheriff Jeff,"
he said, watching Jeff's face in the car's reflected lights,
"but somebody ought to be on duty at the jailhouse."

"Why?" Jeff asked casually.

"Judge Ben Allen might be trying to reach you. If he changes his mind and wants us to do something, he couldn't reach us out here."

Jeff motioned to him to start the car.

They drove slowly away, keeping on the highway for the next mile and a half. They were still nine or ten miles from Andrewjones when Jeff indicated with a motion of his hand that he wanted to turn off the main road and drive up a narrow, rain-washed lane between two fields of knee-high cotton. Bert did not know what Jeff had in mind, but he followed the instructions without comment. He did not recognize the rough winding side-road, but he took it for granted that Jeff knew what he was doing.

They had to ford a creek, but before attempting to cross it, Bert stopped the car.

"Where does this road go, Sheriff Jeff?" he asked anxiously.

"Never mind where it goes to," he said quickly. "Drive on. I know every pig-track in Julie County like I know the inside of my hand. I was over this road only about a week ago, anyway. Drive on."

They forded the shallow stream and bumped over the narrow road for about three-quarters of a mile. From the bottom of a deep gully the car shot up the

171

side of a knoll and jerked to a stop. The road had come to an abrupt end against the side of a dilapidated cowbarn. Beyond the tumbled-down building could be seen the outline of a two-room cabin.

Jeff opened the door and got out before Bert could say anything.

Bert followed Jeff over a single strand of barbed wire that had been strung from the barn to an apple tree at the corner of the yard. The barbed wire was rusty and squeaky to touch. Within the enclosure were scattered the remains of what looked like dozens of old cars in every conceivable stage of wreck. In the light of the bright moon they looked like the bony carcasses of chickens after the flesh had been devoured.

Some of the cars lay on their sides, some were turned completely over like turtles on their backs. Torn remnants of upholstery and rusty pistons and camshafts were strewn on the sandy yard as though they had been hurled from the automobiles and put out of mind. The headlights from the sheriff's car bathed a pile of rusty fly-wheels in a warm red glow.

Jeff was picking his way through the yard.

"What's this, Sheriff Jeff?" Bert asked, running and catching up with him just before he reached the cabin door.

"This is where Sam Brinson lives when he's at home," Jeff said, turning and gazing at Bert in surprise. "I thought everybody knew that."

Jeff went to the door.

"I want to find out if them men turned him loose without me knowing about it."

He knocked on the door.

"Hello!" he called. "Hello!"

There was no sound inside. The windows were closed tightly with wooden shutters, and not even a crack of light showed through the door.

Jeff kicked at the bottom of the flimsy door with his foot. It shook the whole building.

"Hello!" he called louder.

He bent his head forward and listened through a crack. Both of them could hear distinctly the rustling of a cornshuck mattress somewhere inside. A moment later a chair crashed to the floor when it was knocked over.

Jeff stepped back, beaming at Bert.

Presently the door opened an inch, but no more. They could not see anyone.

"That you, Sam?" Jeff asked hopefully, leaning forward and trying to see the dark face through the crack.

"Who there?" a woman's voice asked faintly.

"I want to find out if Sam's home," he said, trying to make his voice sound friendly. "I'm Sheriff McCurtain from Andrewjones."

The door slammed shut, rattling the frame of the whole cabin.

They looked at the door for a moment, and then Jeff rapped heavily on the boards. He stood back and waited, but there was no response.

"Is that Sam's wife?" he asked. "Is that you, Aunt Ginny?"

"How come you want to know that?" she asked suspiciously.

"I'm trying to locate Sam, Aunt Ginny," he answered quickly. "Sam ain't in the jailhouse now."

The door flew open. Aunt Ginny's shining black face was thrust out. She looked at Bert and Jeff suspiciously, grasping the red cotton nightgown tightly over her chest.

"Sam sent me word he locked up in the jailhouse," she stated firmly. She looked at the two white men earnestly. "Ain't he there in it, like he said?"

Jeff shook his head slowly.

"I been studying how to raise me five dollars to bail Sam out of the jailhouse," she said, "but if that man's fooling me, I'm going to lay him low when I catch him." She stopped abruptly, out of breath. Taking a firmer grip on the neck of her nightgown, she leaned forward and looked into the yard. "Ain't no yellow-hided wench going to take my man away from me. When I get my hands on that Sam, I'm going to flail some sense in his head."

"It ain't that exactly, Aunt Ginny," Jeff said, speaking carefully. "It ain't woman-trouble this time. Sam got carried off by some white men. That's why I'm out here looking around for him—"

Aunt Ginny clutched at the door with her free hand. Her eyes looked as if they were turning over in her head.

"Lordy me!" she cried. "Has that man gone and got himself in trouble like that Sonny Clark went and done?"

"It ain't nothing like that," Jeff assured her. "Sam just got carried off by pure mistake, or something."

No one said anything for several moments. Aunt Ginny clutched the red cotton garment tight around her neck and moved backward into the cabin.

Her head suddenly appeared again.

"And it won't about no automobile, either, this time?" she asked unbelievingly.

"No," Jeff told her. "Sam got carried off somewhere in a mix-up. I don't want nothing far-fetched to happen to Sam, and so I came out here looking for him." He backed away from the door. "If he shows up, you tell him I said to let me know right away. I'll be worried about him if he don't show up soon."

"I'll tell him what you said, sheriff," she promised. "I'll tell him them very same words."

They turned and started walking away from the cabin. Aunt Ginny called.

"When is the white folks going to leave the colored be?" she said, turning away before Jeff could answer her.

The door closed, banging shut.

"Hot blast it, I wish folks wouldn't cause me so much trouble," Jeff said. "It looks like people has always got to be stirring up trouble for me. A man my age ought to be at home in bed at this time of night, instead of having to tramp around the country trying to set things right. There ain't a bit of sense in all this to-do."

He walked stiffly through the yard, winding his way between the cars and stepping carefully over piles of rusty fenders and worn-out tires. When he passed the upended body of one of the old cars, he stopped and laid his hand on it for a moment. Scales of rust crumbled in his fingers as he stroked it gently.

"Sam sure does like to have machines around him, don't he?" he said admiringly. "If I was a wealthy man, the first thing I'd do would be to make Sam a present of a machine that would run. He'd be a mighty pleased darky if he had one he could ride around in, wouldn't he?"

Bert nodded, wondering if Jeff was going back to town. It worried him to think that the sheriff's office was untended at a time like this.

He moved up to Jeff's side.

"Judge Ben Allen might be—"

Jeff waved him away brusquely.

"I'm acting on my own, son," he said easily. "I just can't sit by and not try to do nothing for Sam Brinson."

"But—"

"There ain't no 'but' about it, son," he said strangely. "Sam Brinson is a sort of special friend of mine, even if he is a colored man. I just couldn't stand having something bad happen to him."

"What you going to do, Sheriff Jeff?"

"Look for him right up to the last, son," he said, averting his eyes and moving blindly through the yard towards the car.

177

CHAPTER XII

SHEP BARLOW, his pocket sagging with the weight of his pistol, raced down the narrow lane towards Bob Watson's Negro quarters. There were six or seven men at his heels, and the remainder of the crowd was following behind at a slower pace. Shep was in such a hurry to get there he could not wait. He had broken into a run when they climbed the fence a hundred yards away.

The whole straggling crowd of them had cut across the field after leaving the highway three miles from the quarters. They had carefully avoided the road that ran past Bob Watson's house and barns. Bob Watson had lost no time in making it known that he would shoot down the first man who came on his plantation looking for Sonny Clark. Nobody knew where Bob Watson was then, but Shep and his crowd had decided to make a quick raid on the Negro quarters before he could do anything about it. Shep was a brave man when he was with his own crowd, but he had an ingrained fear of his landlord. Bob Watson more than once had threatened to put him off the plantation if he did not take better care of the cotton for which he was responsible.

Shep and the other men slowed down to a walk when they reached the first cabin in the quarters. They tiptoed past several of the dwellings, not knowing which one Sonny lived in. There was not a glimmer of light to be seen in any of the houses; all of them looked deserted. The solid wooden blinds were closed tightly over the windows of every building in the quarters, and, as stealthily investigating fingers discovered, all the doors were locked.

Shep whispered to one of the men beside him, debating which of the dozen or more cabins they should enter first. After only a short delay they decided to choose one at random. All of them moved silently around the building.

When the building was surrounded, one of the men tried the front door. It was locked fast. Drawing his pistol and placing it against the keyhole, he fired. The door swung open without a hitch.

Several men rushed inside, flashlighting the room. The others pushed and shoved until most of them got inside. Others tore open the wooden blinds and climbed through the windows.

A Negro and his wife crouched wild-eyed together on the one bed in the room. They huddled in fright behind the cover of a quilt.

Shep crossed to the bed and jerked the quilt to the floor.

"What's your name, nigger?"

"Luke—"

"Luke what?"

"Luke Bottomly, please, sir," the Negro answered, trembling.

"Where does that nigger, Sonny Clark, live?"

"Who, please, sir?"

"You heard me, you black bastard!" Shep shouted at him, grabbing a gun from one of the men and slamming the stock against his head.

The man crawled to the far corner of the bed, pulling his wife with him.

"Answer me this time," Shep said.

"Sonny Clark lives with his grandmother, Mammy Taliaferro, just a step up the road, white boss, please, sir," he panted.

"Which house?"

"Two houses up that way on the other far side of the road," he said quickly.

All of the men rushed towards the door. Before reaching it, Shep stopped, turned around, and looked at the two Negroes. Half of the crowd had already left the cabin and had reached the road.

"I'm waiting here, I reckon," Shep said loudly. "I'll wait right here to find out if that nigger's telling the truth. I ain't had many niggers to lie to me in my lifetime. It sort of gives me a funny feeling when a nigger lies to me."

Luke and his wife lay shaking with fright in the corner of the bed against the wall. The rickety bedstead squeaked and trembled.

"I'm waiting right here to find out if you lied to me, nigger," Shep said, advancing on the bed. He walked to the foot of it, throwing a beam of light over the dark uncovered body of the woman. "It won't take long to find out," he said, grinning.

Some of the other men were crashing around in the other room, a lean-to that held a cookstove and table.

"Is that your wife there in the bed with you?" Shep asked the Negro.

Luke jerked his head. His lips opened and closed

several times, but no sound came from them. He stared in terror at the faces around him.

"How'd you like somebody to come along and rape her?" Shep asked, grinning at the men around him.

"I'd sure hate that, white boss," he said hoarsely.

"Sure you would," Shep taunted. "It'd make you so mad you'd get yourself a gun and shoot the first sight you got at him, wouldn't you? You'd shoot him down even if he was a white man, wouldn't you, nigger?"

Luke looked appealingly at the white faces around the bed. He shook his head confusedly.

"I wouldn't harm a white man, please, sir," he said low and earnestly.

The girl in the bed cringed, moving closer to him as if begging for protection.

"Where's Sonny Clark?" Shep demanded loudly, holding the beam of light in the Negro's eyes. "Where's he hiding out at?"

"I don't know nothing about Sonny," he pleaded. "Please, sir, I don't."

"You heard about him raping a white girl last night, didn't you?"

"I heard tell about it, but I don't know nothing at

all about it. I ain't seen Sonny since the day before yesterday. That's the truth, white boss!"

One of the men came into the room swinging a board that was the shape of a barrel stave.

"Turn over, nigger," he ordered.

Luke looked pleadingly at the faces of the other men around the bed. He turned slightly, hesitating for a moment.

"Please, sir, white boss, don't do that!" he begged. "I ain't done nothing to be beat about. Please, sir, I ain't!"

"You're a nigger, ain't you?" somebody said.

A man reached over the bed and ripped the Negro's nightshirt from him. He and his wife huddled close together, trying to protect their bodies from the white men.

"White boss, I ain't done nothing to be beat about. I been minding my own business all my life. If I had a beating coming to me, I'd keep my mouth shut. But I ain't done nothing I know about to be beat for. That's the truth, white folks!"

"Keep your mouth shut, nigger, or you'll talk yourself into the worse beating a nigger ever got."

"But, white folks—"

"Turn over like I said!"

He turned over on his stomach, looking around at the faces above him. The board struck him solidly, making a sound that wrung a strangling scream from his wife each time it fell.

"White folks, please have mercy on me!" he cried.

"Shut your mouth, nigger!"

The board filled the room with echoes each time it struck the Negro's body.

After fifteen or twenty hard blows, Luke was ordered to stand up on the floor. He got up and stood cringing by the bed.

One of the men poked the girl's body with the end of a shotgun barrel. She lay with her head buried in the pillow, crying.

"Please, white boss, beat me some more if you want to," Luke said desperately, turning and seeing his wife being poked with the gun, "but don't do nothing to her. She ain't done no wrong. Please, sir, don't do nothing to her!"

"How many times do you have to tell one of these Bob Watson niggers to shut up?" somebody in the crowd said. "It looks like they don't pay no attention at all."

While the woman was being pushed around on the bed with the point of the gun, one of the men went to the mantelpiece over the fireplace and brought back a pint bottle half full of turpentine.

The rest of them crowded around the bed to watch.

"White folks, what you all fixing to do to her?" Luke cried out.

"I told you to keep that God damn mouth of yours shut, didn't I?" Shep shouted, turning and knocking the Negro against the wall with a gun-stock.

The men turned back to the woman. She was forced to stretch out on her back and then the bottle of turpentine was emptied over her stomach. She trembled nervously at first, but as the fluid began to burn her, she screamed with pain. They prevented her from rolling off the bed, and then they stood by and watched her. She was screaming in agony and tearing at herself with her fingernails until her skin began to bleed. Luke tried to go to her, but he was knocked across the room.

All of them were standing by the bed watching the woman writhe and twist when the men who had gone to search the cabin for Sonny came back shaking their heads.

"I don't believe that nigger came home at all last night," one of them said. "Mammy, up there in the cabin, talks like she don't know nothing at all about him. I don't think she's lying. No old nigger woman like her is going to lie about it at a time like this. She's seen too much trouble to let herself get in a fix lying. She said she don't know nothing about Sonny."

The men who had just come back from Mammy Taliaferro's cabin rushed to the bed and watched the Negro woman tossing on it. The odor of turpentine was so strong that they knew without being told what had been done to her. They stood and gaped at her writhing naked body.

Shep was the first to turn and walk away from the bed. Most of the men followed him through the door out into the night. He walked slowly out into the road, looking up and down as though undecided where to look next. His anger was rising. The one thing he hoped to do was to find Sonny before Clint Huff and his crowd could put their hands on him. He was afraid that Sonny would be found somewhere else and lynched before he could do anything about it. The men who had followed him from Luke Bottomly's cabin waited to find out what he was going to do next.

Off in the distance they could hear faint sounds coming from the direction of Needmore. Needmore was a crossroads settlement at the foot of Earnshaw Ridge in the northeast corner of the county. Shep put his hand against his ear and tried to make out what the sound was. He could not detect human voices, and so he did not pay any more attention to it.

Some of the men were walking up and down the road in front of the cabins talking in lowered voices. Shep ran up to one of the dark cabins and kicked down the door. The noise brought everybody running.

"Let's get all of these Bob Watson niggers up and find out what they know," somebody said to Shep.

Shep pushed him away, ignoring the suggestion. He had already made up his mind not to spend much more time in the quarters. He rushed through the door and flashlighted the room with a quick sweeping motion of his hand. Half a dozen other lights were flashed on as the others rushed in.

There was only one person in the cabin, a Negro girl who screamed and tried to hide under a quilt.

Shep jerked off the covering. The girl sat up, her heart pounding with fright.

She was light-skinned and young. She drew her feet under her, edging towards the corner.

The nightgown was ripped from her and tossed aside. Somebody whistled at the sight.

"Where's your man?" Shep asked her, moving closer.

"He's down in the swamp working at the sawmill," she whispered hoarsely.

She looked to be between sixteen and seventeen years old. Her body was slender and round.

"You better not be lying to me," Shep warned her. "How long's he been down at the sawmill?"

"No, sir, I ain't lying," she said, holding her arms tightly around her. "He's been working down there all this year."

"What's his name?"

"Amos Green."

"Don't he never come home?"

"Yes, sir, he comes home every Saturday night always."

"Where's Sonny Clark hiding out at?"

"Who?"

"Sonny Clark. You heard me the first time."

"I sure don't know nothing about Sonny Clark. I ain't seen him at all."

"I didn't ask you if you'd seen him, nigger," Shep said irritably. "I asked you where he's at."

"I don't know where he's at," she answered quickly, almost choked with fear.

Shep turned away and went to the window. As soon

as he had left the bed, the men crowded closer, pushing the girl to the middle of it.

"Do you believe in niggers raping white girls?" somebody asked her.

"No, sir, I don't believe in that," she said.

"You'd want your own man shot down if he raped a white girl, wouldn't you?"

"Amos didn't get in no trouble, did he?" she asked frantically. She looked appealingly at the faces around the bed.

"Why don't you answer what I asked you?" the man said, poking her with his shotgun.

"Yes, sir, I want what you said," she whimpered.

A light suddenly flared up somewhere outside. Shep dashed for the door and ran out. The others ran.

"Something's on fire around here!" one of them said.

When they got outside, they could see flames leaping from a chickenhouse behind the cabin across the road. Some of them ran to it and tried to knock the flaming boards to the ground. By that time it had gained such a start that it was impossible to check it. Most of the men withdrew and watched it burn to the ground. Three or four of them went quietly around the cabin and stepped into the dwelling across the road where they had left the girl a few minutes before. They slipped inside and closed the door noiselessly. No one missed them.

"Who set that fire?" Shep demanded, walking up the road.

Nobody answered him.

"You can't catch a nigger by going around setting fires," he said sourly. "It'll make them run for cover quicker than anything else. Looks like whoever done it would have better sense."

He walked away disgustedly. The crowd watched the chickenhouse burn to the ground, and when the last flame had flickered out, the men moved up the road behind Shep. No one said anything until the Negro quarter was far behind.

"It was getting about time to clamp down on a nigger again," one of the men said. "A week ago I was in a store in Andrewjones, and I'll be damned if a black buck didn't come in with more money in his pocket than I've had in mine all summer long. That made me good and sore, seeing a nigger like him better off than I was. That's the trouble with them these days. They make just as much wages, and sometimes more, than a white man can. Hell, this is a white man's country! Ain't no nigger going to flash a bigger roll of money than I can, and me not do nothing about it. It ain't right."

"Sign that nigger-petition," a voice said from the rear of the crowd. "That's the way to get shed of the niggers."

"I ain't in favor of that fool thing," he retorted loudly. "The best way is just like I said. String one of them up ever so often. That'll make all of them keep their place. Hell, if there wasn't no more niggers in the country, I'd feel lost without them. Besides," he said, turning around and shouting, "who'd do all the work, if the niggers was sent away?"

No one had an answer to his argument. The men walked along in silence, wondering to themselves about a country in which there were no Negroes to do the hard work. No one cared to discuss such a far-fetched possibility.

A mile from the quarters, Shep and three or four men in front of the procession, suddenly stopped in their tracks.

There, unmistakably, stood Bob Watson holding a shotgun pointed at them. The moon gleamed on the metal of the gun, flashing a warning that every one of them understood. No one moved. Bob Watson advanced a few steps.

"I reckon nobody believed what I said," he spoke slowly from behind the gun. "I sent out word that I'd shoot the first one who came on my land looking for Sonny Clark, and I ain't fooling, either. I ain't going to have one of my hands lynched as long as I can stop it. I don't know who all of you men are, but I can see some I recognize. I'd figure that about half of you are my tenants and sharecroppers. That means that the other half ain't got an inch of business being on my land. But that don't excuse the rest of you none."

Somebody in the middle of the crowd spoke up.

"A white girl's been raped, Mr. Bob," he said. "We can't let the niggers overrun the country like that. They've got to be taken care of."

"The sheriff draws a salary to arrest lawbreakers," he said quickly. "Nobody else's got the right to come on my land."

"Hell," one of the men said, "Jeff McCurtain ain't going to hurt his votes by busting in on this nigger hunt. He's got better sense than that."

Bob Watson moved to the side of the road, still holding the gun on the men.

"I'm going to give everybody a chance to get off my land," he said. "This pump gun shoots six times. I'll give everybody a chance to climb through that fence and head for the highway, and then I'm going to start pumping. But I'll warn you. If I catch anybody around here again looking for that boy, I'll shoot on sight next time. And I ain't drawing a line between them who work for me and them who don't. How about that, Shep?"

"Yes, sir, Mr. Bob," he said meekly, moving sideways towards the fence, "I know what you mean."

The crowd broke, dashing out of the road and leaping and falling over the fence. When the last one had reached the other side, Bob Watson emptied the gun into the air. As he took a handful of shells from his pocket with which to reload the gun, he could hear dozens of feet pounding across the field. He stood in the road, holding the loaded gun under his arm, until the sounds had died away in the distance.

CHAPTER XIII

SHERIFF JEFF MC CURTAIN was knee-deep and belly-floundered in a patch of rank pigweed when dawn broke.

The strange-looking country around him was peaceful and quiet. Little wisps of fog were rising from the dew-damp earth and drifting aimlessly over the fallow fields. While Jeff stood gazing at the dawn, a lone shirt-tail woodpecker began hammering happily on a leafless dead sycamore.

Jeff looked around him, wondering where he was. He and Bert had tramped over a lot of strange ground between midnight and daybreak, but for the first time he felt lost. He scratched his head, wondering if he were still in Julie County, or if he had crossed the county line sometime during the night by mistake.

He saw Bert coming towards him from around the corner of one of the old sheds in the barnyard. Bert looked hollow-eyed and wan. His hat had been pushed to the back of his head, and his shoulders drooped despairingly.

"Where in the world are we at, Bert?" he called helplessly. "I don't recall seeing such a ramshackle piece of country since God-come-Wednesday."

"We're only about twelve miles from town," Bert said wearily. "This is Frank Turner's old place."

Bert plodded through the weeds towards him. Jeff felt a little better, knowing that he had jurisdiction over the ground on which he stood. In the early part of his political career he had been subject to nightmares wherein he had found himself floundering helplessly in one of the other counties in the state while murder, arson, and rape were being committed on a wholesale scale right before his eyes. For that reason he had not set foot outside of Julie County in eleven years.

"I don't think Sam Brinson's been here, Sheriff Jeff," Bert said. "I don't think anybody's been on this place in half a dozen years."

They looked at each other hopelessly.

"I wonder what far-fetched thing could have happened to Sam," Jeff said to himself aloud.

"Maybe they turned him loose somewhere and he's too scared to come out of hiding," Bert suggested. "If they got tired of hauling him around with them, they might have done that, or else they—"

"Or else, what?" Jeff asked quickly.

"Well, they might have gone ahead and—and done what they said they was going to do."

"No!" Jeff said emphatically. "Not to Sam. Maybe to any other nigger. But not to Sam Brinson."

Bert turned and waded through the weeds towards the dilapidated dwelling. The car had been left somewhere in front of the house when they drove up in the dark.

Jeff found it difficult to pick his way through the heavy growth of pigweed, but he did the best he could by following the trail left by Bert. When he got as far as the shed, he heard somebody shouting near by. He stopped and listened closely, filled with renewed hope. It might be Sam calling.

Bert had reached the dwelling, but he was coming back.

"It's Jim Couch," he called to Jeff.

Jeff went to the side of the shed and leaned wearily against it.

He could hear Bert and Jim crunching through the weeds, but he did not look up.

"Good morning, Sheriff Jeff," Jim said breathlessly. "It's a fine day, ain't it?"

Jeff did not answer. He wanted a few moments of peace in his mind before hearing what Jim had to say. He knew that if Jim had brought good news he would have shouted it out long before that.

"I've been looking all over Julie County for you and Bert since last night," Jim began. "I reckon I must have asked two or three hundred people if they had seen anything of you. I wouldn't have found you out here at all, if it hadn't been for your car standing up there in front of the house."

Jeff's heart sank lower. He closed his eyes for one more moment of peace.

"What's the trouble, Jim?" he asked finally, opening his eyes.

"Judge Ben Allen—"

Jeff groaned.

"I might have known that," he said, dropping his voice lower. "I've been fearing that all night long."

"Judge Ben Allen had a fight with Mrs. Narcissa Calhoun about that petition," Jim said quickly. "He took it away from her and tore it to pieces and told her he would have her arrested for inciting a riot if she tried to get up another one."

Jeff raised his eyes hopefully, his lower jaw dropping.

"Then he called up and told me to find you right
away and tell you he wanted Sonny Clark caught and
brought to the jailhouse for safekeeping with every
hair in his head where it ought to be."

Jeff slumped against the wall of the shed, his fingers
digging at the rough weatherbeaten boards for support.
He was as pitiful a sight as a month-old calf caught
in a barbed-wire fence.

"Boys," he said dispiritedly, "I haven't been so
frazzle-assed tired since God-come-Wednesday. I been
tramping Julie County all night long trying to find
Sam Brinson, and now along comes Judge Ben Allen,
changing his mind again, and saying he wants me to
drop everything and catch that Clark nigger. It's that
Cissy Calhoun who's made all this trouble. If I could
put my eyes on her now, I'd chase her till she was so
worn-out she'd wish she'd never been born."

He slid slowly down the shed wall, his body making
a thud on the ground. Bert and Jim leaped forward
in an effort to save him from a fall, but they were
unable to reach him in time.

The most pleasant feeling he had ever had in his
whole life came over him. It was the hottest day of

summer, and he was watching Sam Brinson tinker with an old car out in the sun. Sam was hammering away at the rusty old machine while he lay back against the trunk of a long-limbed wateroak tree on the cool bank of Lord's Creek and fished for speckled trout. To lie there in the shade, with the soft cool mud oozing between his toes, and to hear Sam out there tinkering away on the old automobile, was almost too good to be true. He was fishing with worms and a cork, and the cork began to bob. He watched the ripples spread over the water, waiting for the cork to go under twice. Without taking his eyes from the cork, he spread his feet wider apart, pushing his toes deeper into the cool mud. Then he got ready to jerk the line the instant it was pulled under the third time. He set himself then and there to catch six or eight of those man-sized trout, and to take them home for Corra to fry and brown in corn meal. All of a sudden the cork went under for the third time, and he jerked with all his might. He lost his toe-hold in the mud; he slid down the slippery bank into the water; and the fishing pole went soaring out of sight over his head.

He opened his eyes to see Bert and Jim standing over him fanning his face as hard as they could. He closed his eyes quickly, wondering why he had grown to hate fishing the way he did if it was anything at all like that.

"Take it easy, Sheriff Jeff," Bert was saying. "Take it easy, Sheriff Jeff. You'll be all right in a minute. Take it easy, Sheriff Jeff."

"Boys," he said, looking at them strangely, "I hooked the biggest one you ever did see."

"Take it easy, Sheriff Jeff," Bert said, fanning harder and looking at Jim Couch.

"I had some bullies that weighed eight to nine pounds, but I threw them right back because they was too little. The law says to throw back in anything under six inches, but McCurtain ain't never fished for anything that measures, from nose to tail, less than—"

He sat up, looking across the patch of weeds.

"Where's Sam?" he shouted. "Where'd Sam go to?"

"Everything's all right, Sheriff Jeff," Bert tried to assure him. "There's no hurry about nothing. Just take it easy for a while."

No one spoke for a while. Bert and Jim watched him, fanning all the time. The sun had reached the tops of the trees across the fallow field, and rays fell across Jeff's face. He looked up, blinking in the strong light.

"Something must have come over me," he said

sheepishly. "Everybody knows I don't like fishing one bit."

"That's right, Sheriff Jeff," Bert said. "Me and Jim ain't going to believe it. We know you don't like to fish."

He sat quietly for a while, and then he motioned to Bert and Jim to help him to his feet. He got up with difficulty and staggered through the pigweed patch towards the car, pushing the rank stalks aside with a sweeping motion of his hands.

"I'm all right now," he said, warding Bert and Jim off when they attempted to help him to the car. "I'm all right if I didn't make a fool out of myself."

They followed close behind where they could help him if he stumbled on the rough ground.

They opened the car door for him and stood back, waiting for him to say what they were going to do.

"I'm doing my duty as I see it," he said, settling back comfortably in the seat. "If Judge Ben Allen wants a dead nigger, I'll get him. But if he wants a live one, he'll just have to wait till I find out about Sam first, or else he'll have to go out and catch him himself. The cemeteries is full of politicians who didn't heed the voice of the common people, and I don't aim to be carried there before my time."

"You mean we ain't going to look for Sonny Clark?" Jim asked.

"I mean just that, son," he said. "I ain't going to run myself frazzle-assed running first in one direction and next in another. If Judge Ben Allen can't make up his mind and leave it made up, that's a pretty fair sign that he ain't so sure of the will of the common people. That's all I want to know. I'm going to stay straddle the fence till I'm convinced I'll land on solid ground when I leap. In the meanwhile, I've got my eyes open for Sam Brinson. I'll look for him till God-come-Wednesday, if necessary."

"Are we going to start looking some more for Sam toreckly?" Bert asked, hoping the search would be halted long enough for them to find breakfast somewhere.

"No," Jeff said firmly, slapping his hand on the car window. "No. We're going to start looking now."

He pointed out the direction he wanted to go, and Bert turned the car around. They drove off in the direction of Needmore with Jim following in the other automobile.

A mile down the road they came to a three-room tenant house perched on the edge of a cotton field. There was a mailbox on a hickory post in front of the dwelling. A man in patched overalls was leaning against the post watching the two cars approach.

"Slow up, Bert," Jeff said, nudging him in the ribs. "Maybe this bugger knows where Sam went to. Stop the car."

The car rolled to a stop a few feet from the farmer. He looked up suspiciously, pulling his sun-scorched field-straw hat down over his forehead.

"Howdy," Jeff greeted him, leaning out the window and wrinkling his face in a grin.

"Howdy," the man replied.

They looked at each other closely, each waiting for the other to speak first after that. Jeff realized after several moments that it was up to him to say something.

"Hot weather we've been having lately, ain't it?" he said.

"I reckon so."

"How's your woman and all the young ones?"

"Fair."

"Laid-by yet?"

"Not yet."

"Figuring on taking a government loan on your cotton this fall?"

"Ain't decided."

"Did the boll weevils hurt your crop much?"

"Not much."

"It's hot, ain't it?"

"Yeh."

The two men watched each other suspiciously, each trying to fathom the other's mind. The farmer took out his pocketknife and whittled several strokes on the mailbox post. Jeff drew in a long deep breath and leaned farther out the window.

"Who you going to vote for this coming election?" he asked, unable to withhold the question any longer.

"I'm a Democrat."

"Anti-Judge Allen, or pro-Judge Allen?"

"I ain't no Allen-Democrat, if that's what you're driving at," the farmer said heatedly, pushing his hat away from his forehead and spitting a stream of tobacco juice at the front tire.

Jeff leaned back and ran his hand over his face, relieved to know the kind of ground he was on. He made a sign to Bert to switch off the motor.

"I'll be running again myself this year, as usual," he said, tilting back his hat and smiling at the man against the post. "I've got a mighty clean record in back of me. I've devoted the best part of my life to being the servant of Julie County voters, but I've made it a hard and fast rule never to treat the Allen-Democrats to political favors when it comes to up-holding the laws—"

"What's your name?" the farmer asked, spitting at the front tire and straightening up.

"Me?" Jeff said, taken back. "Why, I'm Sheriff Jeff McCurtain. I thought—"

"How come you didn't lock up that nigger in the jailhouse?"

He looked at Jeff, squinting one eye and wiping the knife-blade on the palm of his hand.

"What nigger? You mean Sam Brinson? I had—"

"I don't know nobody by that name. I mean Sonny Clark."

Jeff swallowed hard, glancing at Bert. He was beginning to be afraid that he had done himself more harm than good by stopping and getting involved in politics.

"How come you didn't stir around and catch him before that mob got on his trail?"

"I figured—"

"You draw a good sum of money out of the public funds, don't you?"

"It don't amount to much," Jeff protested. "It ain't no more than a bare living."

"It's a heap more than I make, and I know a lot of folks like me. The county keeps a pair of bloodhounds, too. If you wanted to catch that nigger, all you had to do was let them bloodhounds loose on his trail. Now, ain't that so?"

Jeff opened the door to allow the air to circulate better. The heat was making perspiration break from his flesh like water seeping through a flour sack.

"Now, about them bloodhounds," Jeff spoke up defensively. "Bloodhounds don't always do as much good as some folks think. Anyway, that was such a smart nigger, I figured he'd wade down Flowery Branch, and them hounds wouldn't never be able to strike his trail. On top of that, they'd be yelping so much, he'd be warned away. I figured the best way to catch him was to beat the bush and grab him that way."

"Why didn't you do it that way, then?" the man asked persistently.

Jeff ran his hand over his face nervously. He was at a loss to know how to handle the situation. He sat hoping that there were not many voters in Julie County like the man leaning against the mailbox post. He knew he could not afford, even at that stage, to take a public stand either for or against the lynching until he knew which way the wind was blowing. He dreaded the coming election worse than he did a plague. This was one time when he knew there was no possible way for him to keep from taking a stand on one side or the other, and he knew as well as he knew his own name that his chances of being re-elected were not worth an argument if he failed to gauge correctly the sentiment of the people. In the past, Judge Ben Allen had always been able to settle the outcome of the primaries in advance merely by making a few trades and switches with the opposition. But now Jeff was beginning to wonder if Judge Ben Allen had enough political power to swing an election when the untested issue of lynching was to be brought out in the open for the first time in the history of Julie County. He wished he had had the sense to follow his wife's advice when she told him to go fishing, and to get there as fast as he could travel.

The man in the patched overalls was gazing at him stolidly. Jeff bit his lower lip, hoping the man would not press the unanswered question upon him.

"By the way," Jeff said, attempting to sound as casual as possible under the circumstances, "I don't reckon you've seen anything of Sam Brinson, the colored man, have you?"

The farmer narrowed his eyes, fixing his gaze on the front tire as though he were sighting down a gun barrel, and spat unerringly upon the sidewall of the rubber casing. A few faint lines appeared at the corners of his mouth.

"Who's that? I never heard of him before?"

"Sam's from over on the other side of Flowery Branch—about halfway between the branch and Andrewjones."

The man shook his head slowly.

"Who does he work for?"

"Nobody, exactly," Jeff said apologetically, "except for himself, you might say. He sorts of fools around with old cars that he gets his hands on one way or another."

"Never heard of him," the man said, shaving the post with his knife, "but he sounds like one of them Geechee niggers to me. That breed'll do anything to keep from working in the fields like ordinary niggers."

Jeff was too discouraged to sit there and argue any more. He made a motion at Bert, indicating that he wanted to leave. Bert started the engine.

"If you hear any word about Sam Brinson," Jeff said, raising his voice above the noise of the motor, "I'd appreciate it a heap if you'd let me know."

The farmer did not say anything in reply. He turned over the wad of tobacco in his left cheek with his tongue, but the car rolled away before he could spit on the tire again. They left him standing with his shoulder propped against the mailbox.

They had gone nearly a mile before Jeff spoke.

"I reckon I can count that vote lost till God-come-Wednesday," he said sadly. "How was I to know he'd have it in for Geechee niggers, and not be an Allen-Democrat, besides?" He paused, looking with dismal eyes at the landscape. "There sure are some queer creatures that a politician has to poll."

The road they were on ran north-and-south through the county along the eastern boundary. By following it northward they were not getting any closer to Andrewjones, which lay about fifteen miles to the west at that point, but they were getting closer to Earnshaw Ridge.

During the next twenty minutes they passed half a dozen or more deserted-looking Negro cabins. In the yard of one cabin the week's washing hung on the clothesline, but the dwelling itself looked as if it had been deserted on a few minutes' notice. The wooden shutters had been closed and bolted over the windows, but the front door remained ajar.

"Drive on to Needmore, Bert," Jeff said, pointing ahead. "I want to inquire around for Sam. It stands to reason he's somewhere, now, don't it? He just couldn't be swallowed up in a hole in the ground and not leave a trace of himself behind."

It was Saturday, and ordinarily the roads would have been crowded even at that early hour with Negroes afoot, riding on mules, and driving their old cars. But there was not a Negro to be seen anywhere.

Even in Needmore there were no Negroes to be seen.

Needmore was a crossroad settlement barely large enough to have a name. On opposite corners there were two general stores with high dashboard fronts. One of the stores had a tall red gasoline pump beside it. Other than a handful of scattered, unpainted, white-inhabited bungalows, there was nothing else in the settlement. The place had been given its name by the Negroes who went there to trade at the stores, and who were usually told, when they attempted to purchase an article, that they would need more money.

Bert slowed down the car and stopped in front of the store with the gasoline pump. Jim Couch drew up beside them almost at once.

Jeff gazed out upon the barren sandy soil around the stores, unable to stop worrying. He felt too tired to get out of the car, so he sent Bert to bring his bottle of Coca-Cola out to him.

CHAPTER XIV

H ARVEY GLENN, a young cotton farmer who lived
on the panlevel on top of Earnshaw Ridge, was
coming down the path from his house after breakfast
that morning chewing a toothpick in the corner of his
mouth when he saw a Negro's woolly head sticking
out of a clump of murdock weeds. Harvey stopped,
tossed the toothpick aside, and looked around for a
rock.

While he was searching the ground for a stone the
size he wanted, the waist-high weeds shook a little.
The woolly head dropped out of sight.

Harvey stepped back, looking hurriedly all around
him for a rock of any size.

The night before, when word of the man-hunt had
spread over all the countryside, Harvey went to bed
with his wife as usual. At least half of the men in that
end of Julie County went out on the hunt, but Harvey
told his wife, who was afraid of being left alone in the

house, anyway, that nobody had the right kind of eye-sight to catch a Negro in the dark, and that he was not going to waste any of his time trying.

As soon as he had eaten his breakfast that morning, though, he put on his hat and started down the ridge. He was about halfway between his house and the road at the bottom when he happened to glance off to one side and saw the murdocks shaking.

"Is that you, Sonny?" he called, stooping down and picking up a field stone about the size of a brick.

The weeds shook violently, but there was no answer.

"You heard me, Sonny," he said, raising his voice.

He thought he heard a faint sound. It was like a moan trailing off into a whimper.

"What's the matter out there?" he called, craning his neck.

Harvey took several steps into the weeds, stopping and rising on his toes in an effort to see if it really was Sonny Clark crouching out there. He was careful not to take too much of a chance until he could be sure it was Sonny, because he had left his rifle with his wife for her protection.

"You'd better answer me, Sonny!" he said impatiently.

There was no motion in the weeds, and the woolly head had disappeared completely from sight.

"Stand up on your feet, Sonny!" he ordered, moving closer. "Stand up and let me see you, or I'll chunk this rock right spang at you!"

Sonny's head rose to the top of the murdocks like a turtle warily emerging from its shell. His eyes became larger and larger as he got to his feet.

"Howdy, Mr. Harvey," Sonny said. "How you, today?"

Harvey pushed through the weeds towards the boy, stopping and staring at him when he was a few feet away.

"What you doing in my field, nigger?" he said gruffly, moving around him in a circle in order to see if Sonny had a weapon of any kind.

Sonny's body turned as though it were on a pivot, his large round eyes following every movement of Harvey's legs.

"Is this here your field, Mr. Harvey?" Sonny asked, his voice rising in surprise. "I declare, Mr. Harvey, I didn't know this here field belonged to you at all. I thought maybe it didn't belong to nobody, because on account of all these here weeds—"

"All land belongs to somebody or other," Harvey stated flatly.

"Is that right?" Sonny said, his voice trailing off vaguely. "I didn't know that before, Mr. Harvey."

"You know it now," he said quickly, stopping and facing the boy. "What you doing hiding out in it like this?"

"Yes, sir, Mr. Harvey. I knows whose it is now, all right." He paused and looked down at the weeds. "I just don't know how come I got to be in it like I is, though."

"Why ain't you at home working? Ain't you one of Mr. Bob Watson's field-hands?"

"Yes, sir," Sonny said eagerly, "I live on Mr. Bob's place." He looked around behind him, searching the horizon with a sweep of his eyes. "I just didn't feel like working today, somehow. I ain't feeling at all well, Mr. Harvey."

Harvey threw down the rock and strode into the circle of trampled-down weeds where Sonny had been crouching. It looked to him as if Sonny had been there a long time, possibly all night. The boy backed away several steps, his quick darting eyes taking in most of the horizon with a swift glance.

"What makes you feel like not working?" Harvey

asked him. "You ain't been getting into trouble of no kind, have you?"

Sonny's face twitched. He swallowed hard. His hands dug deep into the pockets of his tattered overalls.

"Mr. Harvey, I ain't done no wrong," he said earnestly. "I declare, I ain't!"

"What about that raping?" Harvey demanded quickly. "You don't call that wrong?"

Sonny's face fell.

"Does you know about that, Mr. Harvey?"

"Of course, I know about it. Everybody in Julie County knows about it. People all over the country know about it now after reading about it in the newspapers."

"The newspapers?" Sonny repeated. "Did they put it in the newspapers?"

Harvey nodded, watching the boy.

"I ain't done nothing like that, Mr. Harvey."

Harvey reached down and broke off a handful of weed tops. He rubbed them in the palms of his hands until the seed crumbled from the pods and dribbled between his fingers. He threw the chaff aside and looked at Sonny.

"You done something," he said finally. "What do you call it then?"

"I didn't do that thing you mentioned, Mr. Harvey," he said earnestly, stepping forward and almost stumbling in his haste. "I don't know nothing about that thing you mentioned. I ain't never done nothing like that in all my life, Mr. Harvey. I just ain't, that's all."

"Mrs. Narcissa Calhoun said you did. And she's a white woman. You wouldn't call a white woman a liar, would you?"

"No, sir, Mr. Harvey," he protested. "I sure wouldn't. But I didn't do nothing at all, Mr. Harvey."

"She said she and Preacher Felts saw you doing it. Mr. Shep Barlow's daughter said you done it, too. You wouldn't call all of them liars, would you?"

"I ain't calling them that, Mr. Harvey. I wouldn't dispute white-folks' word for nothing in the world. But I just naturally didn't do nothing like that to Miss Katy, or to nobody else, Mr. Harvey."

Sonny was going around in a circle, stumbling and catching himself almost every time he took a step. He was trotting in a nervous haste to convince Harvey of his innocence. Harvey stood still, looking closely at the boy's agonized face each time he passed in front of him.

"I'm telling you the truth, Mr. Harvey, when I said that. I ain't never done nothing with colored girls, either. I just don't know nothing about that, Mr. Harvey."

Harvey watched him closely. He could not keep from his mind a surging belief in the Negro's earnestness.

"How come you said that about colored girls, too?" he asked. "You never had dealings with one of them, either?"

"No, sir, Mr. Harvey. That's the truth. I've heard talk about it, but I never got around to knowing about it. I wouldn't tell you no lie, Mr. Harvey."

Harvey turned his back on the boy and walked in the direction of the path a dozen yards away. When he reached the bare strip of sandy ground, he stopped and looked down the path and over the tops of the trees at the bottom of the ridge. Beyond that lay the flatlands crisscrossed with hedgerows separating the fields of growing crops. He wondered where the crowd of men was. He had not heard the men since the evening before when there was a lot of shouting at the bottom of the ridge.

He turned around and looked at Sonny standing waist-deep in the murdocks. The boy was standing in the same position he had left him in. He had made no signs of running away. Harvey walked back to where he stood.

"What you aim to do, Mr. Harvey?"

"I don't know," he said.

Harvey thought he detected a movement under Sonny's shirt. He moved closer.

"What's that you've got hid?"

Sonny unbuttoned his shirt and put his hand inside. He drew out the rabbit.

"Where'd you get that rabbit?"

"It's just one of mine," Sonny said, stroking the rabbit's ears. "I got him from home night before last, Mr. Harvey."

Sonny held the rabbit by the ears, resting the animal's body on his forearm. The rabbit struggled for a moment in an effort to get down and nibble the grass that grew sparsely in the weeds. Sonny put him back into the blouse of his shirt and buttoned it.

"I don't know," Harvey said uneasily, pulling his hat hard over his eyes. "I just don't know."

"What don't you know, Mr. Harvey?" the boy asked helpfully.

219

Harvey did not answer him. He went back to the path and looked down the ridge for a long time. Sonny did not move from his tracks.

It was difficult for him to make up his mind. First he would tell himself that he was a white man. Then he would gaze at Sonny's black face. After that he would stare down upon the fields in the flatlands and wonder what would happen after it was all over. The men in the hunt-hungry mob would slap him on the back and praise him for having captured the Negro single-handed. But after the boy had been lynched, he knew he would probably hate himself as long as he lived. He wished he had stayed at home.

"Mr. Harvey," Sonny inquired plaintively.

He turned on his heel angrily.

"Mr. Harvey, please, sir, let me hide away up at your house. I'll get in the barn and do just like you say. Please, sir, Mr. Harvey, don't make me go down where that crowd of white men is!"

That settled it. He could not let himself hide a Negro while half the white male population of Julie County was turning the country upside down in search of him.

"Come on," he said roughly, beckoning to Sonny. "Come on this way."

He started down the path. After taking several steps he heard Sonny at his heels. He did not turn around.

They walked down the winding path towards the highway at the foot of the ridge. It was about half a mile from where they had started down to the point where the path ended at the road. Harvey did not turn around to look at Sonny until they were more than half the way down. He could hear the sound Sonny's bare feet made when they rustled a dry leaf or twig in the path. The rest of the time there was nothing to indicate that he was following as he had been told to do.

They stopped at the edge of a clearing. Several automobiles had raced along the dusty highway, coming and going in nervous spurts of speed. The dust hung like a pall over the road.

Harvey turned on his heels and looked Sonny straight in the eyes.

"Why did Mrs. Narcissa Calhoun say you done it, if you didn't do it?" he demanded angrily. "She wasn't the only one who said it, either. Two others said the same thing."

Harvey was angry, but he did not know what had made him feel that way. He watched Sonny's face.

"Mr. Harvey," Sonny said earnestly, "I don't know

why the white folks say I done it when I didn't. I was walking along the road minding my own business when Miss Katy ran out of the bushes and grabbed me. I didn't know what she done it for. I thought she was clear out of her mind. She started in saying she wasn't going to tell on me. I tried to ask her what it was she wasn't going to tell on me about, but she wouldn't listen to nothing I said. All that time I knowed good and well I didn't have no business standing there like that talking to a white girl, but I couldn't do nothing about it. She grabbed hold of me and wouldn't leave go. And she wouldn't pay me no mind at all. I tried to get away from her, but she grabbed tighter till I couldn't do nothing. Every time I made a move, she jerked me like I don't know what. I wanted—"

"Did she know who you was?"

"Yes, sir. She knowed I was Sonny, because she kept on calling me by my name. Right then is when Mrs. Narcissa Calhoun and Preacher Felts drove up in the car and stopped right beside us. Miss Katy never did say I was harming her. Miss Katy didn't say nothing. But she acted like she wanted to run, just like I did. Then that white woman grabbed her and wouldn't let her. And Preacher Felts knocked me down on the ground and kept me there. Then that white woman made Miss Katy say it. She made her keep on saying it, too. Then she told Preacher Felts to let me run off, but she kept a hold on Miss Katy and wouldn't let her run. That's what happened, Mr. Harvey. If the Good Lord Himself was here to speak for me, that's what He'd tell you, Mr. Harvey. And you knows good and well He wouldn't lie, don't you, Mr. Harvey?"

Harvey looked away, taking his eyes from the boy. He did not know what to think. He was more convinced than ever, though, that Sonny should not be held responsible for what had happened. If Sonny had been a few years older, or if he had been in trouble before, he knew he would not hesitate an instant. He'd drag Sonny to a tree and tie him up until he could get word to the crowd that had already spent two nights and a day looking for him.

"If I don't turn you over to the white men who've been combing the country for you ever since day before yesterday, they'll call me a nigger-lover when they find out I turned you loose." He hesitated, digging the soft sand with the toe of his shoe. "They might even be apt to run me out of the country. Them men down there has set their heads on stringing you up, and I don't know nothing in the whole wide world that'll stop them from now on."

"What you say, Mr. Harvey?" Sonny asked, perplexed.

He turned his head sharply in order that he would not have to see the boy's pleading eyes.

Without looking behind, Harvey started down the path, leaping over a ditch into the field and hurrying through the scrawny growth of broomsedge and rabbit-tobacco. Sonny clung at his heels less than a yard behind.

He crossed the narrow untilled field and stopped. Sonny was beside him, looking up at his face. Harvey's head hung in silence for several moments before he could bring himself to speak.

"I hate like the mischief to have to do it, Sonny," he began, trying his best to look the colored boy in the face when he said it, "but this is a white-man's country. Niggers has always had to put up with it, and I don't know nothing that can stop it now. It's just the way things is, I reckon."

Sonny did not say anything, but his eyes rolled around until the whites looked like fresh bolls of unstained cotton. He had grasped the meaning of what Harvey had said.

They went on towards the road, ducking their heads under the low-hanging branches in the hickory thicket and picking their way carefully through the briars on each side of the path.

"Mr. Harvey," Sonny whispered in a low voice.

Harvey stopped and turned around. He knew he had made up his mind, but he did not know what he would do if the boy suddenly darted into the thicket.

"What you want, Sonny?"

"Mr. Harvey, won't you please, sir, do one little thing for me?"

"What?"

Sonny stepped forward, pushing back the branches with his strong black arms, and looked at him pleadingly.

"Mr. Harvey, if you thinks you has got to go do what you says, I'd be mighty much obliged if you went and shot me down with a gun instead of turning me over to all them white men."

Harvey could not find words to utter. He looked at the boy strangely, feeling that he had never seen him before in all his life. Then his eyes were no longer able to see what he was looking at, and he turned away. His feet moved along the path, carrying him with them.

"Won't you do that, Mr. Harvey?"

"I couldn't, Sonny."

"Why, Mr. Harvey?"

He shook his head from side to side, every muscle in his neck aching painfully.

"Why, Mr. Harvey?" Sonny repeated pleadingly.

"I ain't got a gun to do it with," he said, stumbling over the ground.

CHAPTER XV

I<small>T WAS</small> barely mid-morning when Jeff and Bert drove away from Needmore, but the day had already seemed to Jeff to be the longest one he had ever had to endure. Jim Couch had been sent back to Andrewjones with a vaguely worded message for Judge Ben Allen. After a night of fatiguing wandering, sleepless and hungry, Jeff had resigned himself to his fate. However, tucked away in a corner of his mind, there was the hope that by some miracle he would find himself re-elected when the votes were counted.

They drove along the road in silence. The unpaved surface was rough and bumpy, and occasionally they ran into washboardy stretches that rattled and shook the car until it sounded as if it would fall to pieces. When Jeff could stand it no longer, he told Bert to slow down.

"I'll bet there've been more cars over this road in the past two days than there have been in the whole year since January," Bert said.

"I'll remind the road commissioner to send some grading machines out here and work it over after this lynching business is finished."

Just then, rounding a curve in the road, they almost ran into a man riding muleback. He was a farmer going to one of the stores in Needmore with a basket of eggs to trade.

Bert stopped the car just in time. The farmer, with only one free hand, was unable to make the slow-moving mule turn to the side of the road. Bert pulled over to one side.

"Howdy," the man said, pulling the mule to a stop. "You're Sheriff McCurtain, ain't you?"

"Howdy," Jeff said, forcing a smile to his face. "I reckon I am the sheriff. Leastaways, till election-time. If I got the votes of a lot of fine-looking farmers like you, I reckon I'd keep on being. How you voting this year?"

"Ain't decided yet," the man said, shifting the egg basket from one hand to the other. "I'll have to do some weighing in my mind, like I always do before I cast my ballot."

"Well," Jeff said, forcing the smile to both sides of his face, "I always admire a voter for talking that way. The people ought to make sure of the politician they

228

put into office. A lot of times the wrong kind of man gets elected, and the common people suffer."

The farmer nodded. He changed the basket of eggs back to his other hand.

"I saw a peculiar thing a little while ago," he turned and jerked his head down the road behind him, "about half a mile back. I was going to mention it when I got to Needmore."

"What did you see?" Jeff asked, sitting up.

"A nigger," he said. "It's a funny thing, but I saw a nigger I'd never seen around here before. He looked like one of them Geechee niggers to me. But the peculiar thing about it was that it was any kind of nigger. It's the first one I've seen since the day before yesterday when every last one of them around here struck out for the deep woods."

"Where'd he go to?" Jeff demanded, almost rising off the seat. "Where's he at now?"

The farmer shook his head.

"He was standing back there in a little clearing beside the road when I saw him first. He acted like he was in a sort of daze, and he didn't run off at all. I said something to him, but he acted like he didn't hear me. That's the thing that struck me as peculiar. I ain't never seen a nigger act like that before."

Jeff began nudging Bert with his elbow, at the same time thrusting his body to and fro as though he were trying to make the car begin rolling before the engine was started.

"I've got to go see about that!" he shouted at the farmer. He nudged Bert hard in the ribs. "Hurry, Bert! Hurry!"

They raced down the road with no thought about the roughness of the surface. Jeff clung to the door with both hands. Every once in a while he turned and looked at Bert with an impatience he could not control.

"That's Sam, all right," he said excitedly. "It never was nobody else but Sam. That's pure Sam, all right!"

They were traveling at a speed of fifty miles an hour, but it still was not fast enough to suit Jeff. He nudged Bert hard in the ribs again.

"You know what I'm going to do, Bert?" he said, his eyes glazed with nervousness.

"What, Sheriff Jeff?"

"I'm going to get the court to issue a writ of *non compos mentis* for Sam. Then he won't always be getting plagued with attachments. He'll have all the leeway in the world, and can fool with the old automobiles as much as he wants to, but he can't be held responsible for his acts. That's what I'm going to do! I'm going to get that writ as soon as I get back to town!"

Bert jammed on the brakes, bringing the car to a screaming stop. Ten feet away stood Sam Brinson, gazing at them perplexedly. Jeff leaped out as fast as he could. Sam's body shook as though he were coming down with chills-and-fever. His overalls were so ripped and torn that they looked as if they had been pieced together out of rags.

"Hot blast it, Sam, where in the world have you been all this time!" Jeff shouted, throwing his body forward and plunging through the roadside weeds.

Sam dived into the thicket behind him. He was out of sight in an instant.

"Sam!" Jeff called, thrashing blindly in the wiry tangle. "Wait a minute, Sam!"

Bert ran up to Jeff's side.

"Stand still and be quiet, Sheriff Jeff," Bert said. "Maybe we can hear him."

They listened intently, twisting their necks and parting the foliage carefully.

"Is that you, Mr. Jeff?" a thin, frightened voice asked.

"It's me, Sam! There ain't nothing to be scared about now. Come on out!"

They waited, but Sam did not appear.

"You heard me, you black rascal!" Jeff shouted impatiently. "Come on out before I turn loose and shoot you out. I'm looking straight at you. You can't hide from me."

The bushes began to shake twenty feet away. Sam came forward inch by inch.

"Where you been all this time, Sam?"

"Mr. Jeff, don't ask me. Just ask me where I ain't been. I declare, I never had so much disturbance in my whole life before."

He cringed, stooping, before them. His eyes were bloodshot.

"I thought sure you was done for," Jeff told him. He was so glad to see the Negro that he felt like going up to him and feeling him to make sure he was real and alive. "I been looking all over for you," he said with pretended gruffness. "Where you been?"

Sam began to tremble as the memory of the past several hours came over him.

"Mr. Jeff, them white men just near about ran me down to skin and bones." He looked down at his feet. The soles of both shoes were missing, and the uppers hung around his ankles. "They chased me through the thickets with a rope tied around my neck, and when they got tired doing that, they tied me to the back end of a car and pulled me along that-a-way. Half the time they went so fast I couldn't keep up, and I dragged on the ground. I thought my time had come for sure until a little while ago when they found that Sonny Clark and let me go."

"Found him?" Jeff shouted at the Negro.

"Yes, sir, Mr. Jeff. They done found him and let me go. That was a while back, and I reckon that black boy is done for by now."

"Where?" he demanded.

"Back down the road there at the branch where them willow trees is at."

Jeff took out his watch and studied the face. He pushed his thumbnail against the crystal as though he were trying to move the hands forward.

"It's getting late in the morning," he said, glancing up at the sun for comparison. "It ain't much longer till dinner-time."

Jeff put his watch away and started for the car. Bert walked along beside him.

"Mr. Jeff," Sam said meekly, "what you aim to do about me?"

They turned around and saw him backing into the thicket.

"Come on here, you black rascal," Jeff said. "I don't ever want to find you getting out of my sight again. Get in the car. I'm going to put you back safe in the jailhouse."

They all got in. Sam crouched down on the floor in the rear instead of sitting on the seat.

After going two or three miles, Sam called in a low voice.

"What do you want, Sam?" Jeff asked.

"I forgot to tell you about the rabbit."

"What rabbit?"

"I don't exactly believe it my own self," he said haltingly, "but I saw it."

"Saw what?"

"When them white men grabbed Sonny, a rabbit jumped out of his shirt, just like it was coming out of his belly. But it hadn't hopped more than a couple of hops before they fired away at it and blasted it all to bits. Now, Mr. Jeff, I don't want you to believe it, because I don't exactly believe it, either. But my eyes saw it."

Bert's and Jeff's eyes met, but neither of them spoke. Jeff twisted his body on the seat and looked down at Sam crouching on the floor. He turned around after that and kept his eyes on the road ahead.

Just before they reached Flowery Branch bridge, two cars came up the road and roared past in a cloud of choking yellow dust. They were going so fast it was impossible to identify any of the men.

"It looks like they've finished, just like Sam said," Bert commented.

"If they've actually gone ahead and pure done it, I'm thankful I saved one out of the two," Jeff said.

A hundred yards from the bridge they saw dozens of automobiles standing in the road, blocking it, and others turned out into the weeds on the roadside.

Jeff's hand on Bert's arm brought the car to a stop. A moment later he motioned to Bert to drive the car off the highway where it would not be readily observed. Sam looked up over the back of the seat anxiously when he could feel no more motion. He ducked down again, moaning.

"We can't do nothing without some help," Bert said excitedly. "We'd better go to town and deputize—"

"Ain't no need for that now," Jeff said. "They've done done it, son."

Bert drove the car into a thicket until it was practically out of sight of the road. Jeff got out and peered through the bushes towards the grove of willow trees on the bank of the stream.

"They've done it, just like I said," he whispered to Bert beside him.

They could see the body of the Negro boy swinging lifelessly from a limb that had been stripped leafless by bullets and shells. There were still at least forty or fifty men standing in small groups around the tree. Others were leaving. One or two cars could be heard to start near the bridge.

"The only thing to do now is send the coroner out here," Jeff said sadly. "There ain't a thing we can do now, son."

Bert caught his arm.

"Maybe we'd better take down a few names," he said, "in case Judge Ben Allen wants to have a case made out."

Jeff was startled.

"No," he said firmly. "I don't want to get mixed up in this thing politically. The people—"

"But—"

Jeff went towards the car, leaving Bert in the bushes. In a few moments he heard Bert calling him in a loud whisper.

"Come here quick, Sheriff Jeff," he called.

Jeff went back to see what he wanted with him.

"Look!" Bert pointed in the opposite direction, downstream.

Katy Barlow was wading through the branch from the other side. None of the men around the tree had seen her then, but she was already less than a dozen yards from them. Then she stopped and looked up at the body of Sonny as it turned slowly on the rope.

"He didn't do it!" she yelled at the top of her voice. The sudden burst of sound in the quiet woods echoed for almost a minute. She ran forward. "It was a lie! He didn't do it! Mrs. Narcissa Calhoun made me say it! He didn't do it!" She was screaming hysterically by the time she had finished.

Men who had gone as far as the bridge came running back to the tree. The ones who were already there stood as if they were in a trance.

Bert could hear Jeff swallow half a dozen times.

"Why don't you believe me!" Katy cried, running from group to group and beating the men with her fists. "He didn't do it! Nobody done it! It was a lie!"

The body on the rope stopped turning for a moment, and then it began to turn slowly in the opposite direction. Some of the men looked up at it, gazing upon it as though they had not seen it before.

"Nobody done it!" Katy screamed. She was disheveled and mud-stained, looking as if she had been struggling through the swamp all night. "It was a lie, I tell you!"

The men had gathered in a semicircle around her, almost shutting her from view. Neither Jeff nor Bert could see her for a while.

"Ask Leroy Luggit!" she cried. "He knows it's a lie! Ask him! Leroy knows!"

She dashed to the tree from which the boy's body hung. The men moved over the ground, keeping up with her.

"Why don't you go find Leroy Luggit and ask him!" she cried hoarsely at the men. "He'll tell you it was a lie! He knows! He knows! He knows!"

There was a period of silence everywhere in the woods. The only sounds Jeff and Bert could hear was the rasping noise in their own throats. The men began to move closer to the tree, and Jeff and Bert were able to see only glimpses of her between the moving bodies.

A piercing scream filled the woods. A roar of angry voices followed. A bluejay fluttered recklessly through the branches of a tree overhead and, screeching shrilly, disappeared in the direction of Earnshaw Ridge.

"What's going on, Bert?" Jeff whispered, shaken.

"I can't see a thing," Bert said helplessly.

"If she's in danger, we'll have to protect her," Jeff said, pausing. "But they wouldn't harm her, would they, Bert?"

Bert hesitated, gripping a sapling in his hand.

"It don't seem like they would," he said. "Unless they've turned on—"

Jeff braced himself against the strongest of the young trees. Perspiration was dripping from his forehead and face.

Katy screamed again, but the sound was faint and weak. The men, as quickly as they had gathered, ran towards the bridge, pushing and cursing each other. For the first time Jeff and Bert saw stones flying through the air. Then, as one final fragment of rock hit her, she sank to the ground without a sound.

Jeff grabbed Bert by the arm, wavering on his feet. Neither of them could speak.

One of the men suddenly turned, ran back, and heaved a heavy stone at Katy's inert body. He raced to the bridge, looking back over his shoulder.

"Bert—" Jeff managed to say.

They moved through the bushes as the noisy sound of automobile motors crashed through the grove. Bert reached the tree long before Jeff could get there. He had fallen on his knees and lifted Katy and was holding her in his arms when Jeff stopped against the tree.

"Katy—" Bert said, holding her as tenderly as he could.

She opened her eyes and looked up at them through her matted raven hair. Bert brushed it away from her face.

A faint smile appeared on her lips.

"Tell Leroy—" she said feebly.

The smile faded away.

Bert laid her down on the pile of stones as gently as he could, and stood up, his eyes searching Jeff's face.

"Sheriff Jeff, her head felt like—" he stopped, looking queerly at the older man. "Her head—"

Jeff nodded, turning his face away. He walked to the bank of the branch and stood looking at the water swirling under a fallen log.

When he turned and looked towards the tree, he saw Bert standing dazedly beside the girl's body, while, above, the darker body turned slowly around and around on the end of the rope. Jeff drew his hand over his face, rubbing his burning eyes.

He left the branch where he had been standing.

"It ought to put an end to lynching the colored for all time," he said, walking away.

Bert ran and caught up with him.

"What did you say, Sheriff Jeff?"

"Nothing, son," he said a little more distinctly. "We got to hurry to town and make a report of this. The coroner will want to know about it. It's his duty to inquire into the cause of deaths like this. He'll want to know all about it in order to be able to perform his duty as he sees it, without fear or favor."

He walked blindly towards the road.

"That's a mighty pretty oath for a man in public office to swear to," he said aloud. "I reckon I had sort of forgotten it."

He walked ahead, alone.